Anush Ravindranathan

An Oral and Maxillofacial Surgeon, he is settled in Kerala with his parents, wife and son, Ayan.

email   : ranush16101986@gmail.com

FB Page : @anushwrites

Blog   : anushravindranathan.wordpress.com

Samsara
(Novel)
English Language
By: Anush Ravindranathan

First Edition
January 2020

All rights reserved

Lay-Out, Cover
Chris Graphics

Printed at
Anaswara Offset, Kochi

Publishers

Saikatham Books LLP
P. B. No- 57
XXV/1230, Chanthiyathu Building,
Kothamangalam P.O., Kothamangalam
Ernakulam Dist., Kerala State,
India. PIN : 686691
LLPIN - AAI-5162
Phone: 0091-9539056858, Office: 0091-485-2823800
email: books@saikatham.com
www.saikathambooks.com

ISBN - 978-93-89463-16-3

₹ 160.00

SAMSARA

Reflections of a Life…
(Novel)

Anush Ravindranathan

Saikatham Books

Preface

Sitting in the hall of our rented house, I was watching news on television with my pregnant wife, Bindiya, by my side. In between, I was looking at my phone, reading and replying to a few congratulatory and critical messages and reviews of my first book, Born Again.

"Why do people kill themselves?" she asked me out of the blue.

"Hmm?" I didn't pay much attention.

"Why do people commit suicide? I mean, what goes through their mind just before they take their lives?" she looked at me. I remember her eyes, they were blank.

"Nobody knows. They don't tell their stories after death, and those who survive the temptation, well, they are the brave ones who don't belong to the earlier said category."

"I disagree. Do you have the courage to hurt yourself even with a pin? If they could overcome that one moment of thought, maybe they will not try again? Or maybe they will? God knows."

"Strong boys don't think about suicide, they overcome the hurdles."

"Again you are wrong Mr Author. The male to female ratio in India is 2:1," she turned the screen of her phone towards me. She was referring to statistics on Wikipedia.

"This is neither the time nor the state when you should think about such topics," I closed the tab.

But, the conversation remained with me. What goes through the mind of a person who commits suicide? Nobody would know. Sometimes, it's a momentarily setback or sometimes it may be a result of accumulation of insults. All they might need is a second thought. A ray of hope.

Dedication

I stood on a hill, saw a smooth silky straight road going as far as my eyes could see. I treaded the road. The path that I treaded was crossed at different junctions by a few mud tracks, which had imprints of many familiar feet. The views around me were so beautiful that I lost my focus, and stumbled upon a rock; I fell down. After few yards, again I slipped down a slope. Then came an uphill part. I wondered, where was the smooth road?

I decided to turn around and seek asylum in one of the beautiful safe havens where I had rested along the path. I turned around. To my astonishment, there was no road, only a few reflections of my past journey were seen. I had two options: to sit down and stay stagnant or to move forward taking the uphill road.

Being restless, I decided to keep moving. The road led me to many beautiful valleys, deep craters, slippery dunes, unseen waters, unknown tastes, mesmerising smells and wonderful creatures. Long way down, I felt too tired to move any more. The road, which I thought was as smooth as silk was never ending, and ever changing. It had no destination but, the journey.

Now, I realise that it is my life, and the restlessness is my spirit that keeps me going.

Dedicated to the journey called life, and the untiring human spirit that keeps it going.

Publishers Note

Anush Ravindranathan is the author of five star rated novel- Born Again. He is an aspiring storyteller who likes to tell stories of human relationships, love, faith, hope and self-belief. Also, he has a critical outlook towards the divisiveness in our society.

'Samsara- Reflections of a Life...' is another humble attempt at touching lives through his stories.

Prologue

Bengaluru; September 8th, 2010.

He came running into their apartment which was no longer 'theirs'. He didn't take the lift; he climbed seven storeys to reach the flat on the eighth floor. He wanted to suffer. He fell and bruised on the way but didn't feel the pain. He was short of breath, his heart beating out of chest. These were trivial when compared to what was going within him.

He stumbled upon nothing as he reached towards the door of the apartment. The key fell off his hands on to the imported tiles flooring the veranda of the posh society where he was living; where he would not have dared to even peek into if it was not for her.

He opened the door and entered the apartment's drawing room. The apartment was no longer well-furnished as it was couple of weeks back, before she had left. His personal stuff accounted for only ten percentage of the furnishing. The remaining were hers, most of which was missing now.

He roamed in the apartment again and again, like a crazy who had lost his shadow, and was searching for it. He searched in all the rooms hoping to find her somewhere. *'May be she was hiding somewhere. May be she was playing a prank on him,'* he hoped, he prayed, and yet he knew it was false. He could not find her anywhere. After what he had learnt about her over the past one week though, he was 'almost' sure, that she was gone forever and would never return.

As if the previous several attempts of his to find her in the vast city over past one week were not enough, his heart wished to make sure one more time 'in case if'.

She was gone. With her was gone his desire to live. He had lost everything that he had, loved, possessed and believed to be his, in a matter of few weeks. It wasn't even 3 weeks since his mother parted the world. And now he stands here alone. Very alone, losing love of his life and all his entire life's savings.

Everything was just an illusion, *a Maya*. He didn't feel like living in this world anymore. This world has ill-treated him enough. He decided to put an end to it one last time.

Was he a coward? No, he was a fighter. He had always been a fighter. Since childhood he had fought against his main opponent, 'his fate', with great zeal to reach where he was now. Where he was now? He himself had never realised or appreciated. God, if there were any, and life had been unfair to him. His miseries and efforts never matched what he had achieved in his life. He had two choices- he could either continue fighting or could altogether quit. The decision was his to make and he didn't want his destiny to decide on it. He had decided. The decision was not 'just' because a girl had left him but an accumulation of all the pain until then. It was his way to show the middle finger to this audacious world, the destiny, the non-existing God and Ramesh; to tell them that they had been impudent to him.

Tomorrow will be his birthday. He would end his life on the very day when it all started at 12:00 AM.

He pressed the power button and his phone beeped to life, it showed 8:55 PM. Let this mobile gifted by her, his first smart phone, guide this ignorant, uncouth, not-so-smart creature through the countdown of his life. He sat on the wooden chair. He decided to write a note or may be a letter, not to blame anyone but let out his agony that had become unbearable. Then, he would cry out loud and jump of the balcony exactly at 12:00 AM. Everything was planned but then, his plans had never worked before.

***

~~Dear~~ God,

I do not know why I am addressing this letter to you? May be because I don't have anyone else to address to or may be because I am fed up blaming myself and want to put it on someone else. But I am not even sure, if you exist. I am sure of one thing though, you are not dear to me and I was never dear to you either.

You know I have decided to bid adieu to my miserable life. Some lives are such, they are given birth to wander without any purpose or destiny. Then they perish into some unknown darkness without anyone noticing, without leaving a mark behind. My life has been one such story. So, without waiting for the destiny to play any more cruel jokes on me, I have decided to take hold of my destiny and end this painful suffering. I am longing to meet my Uppa and tell him how much I had missed his love and protection.

May be the world will consider me a coward. May be the world will say I should have fought harder. May be the world would tag me as a weak soul. May be this decision will reinstate the common belief of all the prejudiced people around me, that I am a loser. May be... but what do they know of me, and why would I even bother of what 'may be's they have about me.

I found no supporting hand when I fell. The only one alive person for whom I was important was my mother. I had left her long back and now, she has left me forever. I never knew or cared if she loved me. But don't know why, I miss her today; at this very moment, I miss her...

I MISS YOU AMMA.

I am going back to her. I promise, I would be a good son up there. I hope, up there she would be exclusively mine and I would take good care of her.

Ramesh, I tried my best to forget him, not to mention him here, but I realise that I still have not forgiven him and never will. He should not have come into our lives as a 'saviour'; he is the destroyer of my peace.

I never knew what I wanted from life. I had no real ambition; just wanted to be rich in some truthful way. I never had any true friends. I spent most of my life earning small and saving large for no real reason. Now, I realise that I don't have anything of my own. Everything I thought I had were never mine.

Maya! I wish I could forget her and move on with my life. But how could I? I failed again. I believed she was the angel that you had sent to guide me out of my miseries. I was so wrong just as I was about Gowri. She made me believe there was something more in me than I had ever thought about myself. I had only one reason to believe that it was true; because Maya said so. Now she is nowhere. All of a sudden, she is no one. I have realised that there are no angels. She was never meant to be in my life and has gone forever.

I thought I would write in this letter about how much hate I have towards you, Maya. But I don't want to lie in these last moments of my life. I LOVE YOU MAYA. I hope and pray for you, to be happy wherever you are and succeed in whatever you do. I want you to achieve every dream of yours, reach all the possible heights of success while you chase your passion. Just a request- please don't ever again step on someone's heart to reach the heights, it hurts a lot.

Why does one live? What gives him the strength to continue? What makes him to carry on? HOPE. A hope that good times will come. A hope that one will succeed. A hope that tomorrow will be definitely be better than what today is. A hope that past could be buried somewhere deep and a new present will blossom over it. Isn't that naive? What happens when one loses that hope? You cease to exist. I too have ceased to exist and I am too tired now- to try, to cry, to shout, to fight or to even breathe.

I QUIT

Never Yours Ever Neglected,

Kuttan

***

Kuttan folded the letter neatly in to four and kept it under the phone. He set an alarm at 11:55 pm. He stared at the door again to make sure no one was watching. He hid himself in the soft furred blanket which she had gifted him. He could not sleep, he lay motionless. He thought of his life until then and wondered if there was something more to his life, beyond what he could see, beyond what he knew.

He had lied about hope. He hoped that the doorbell would ring.

Chapter 1

The Burning Soul

'Tring-trong', rang the doorbell.

An old man in his sixties opened the door. It was Ramesh, Kuttan's ex-*maman*. Ramesh's eye sight had dwindled. Without his glasses, it took much effort to recognise Kuttan. It had been long since Kuttan had visited them; his mother was sick. She wished to see Kuttan for one last time before she could leave this world and thus put an end to her sorrowful life which probably no one understood.

Kuttan was hesitant to meet his mother. It was Maya who had insisted that Kuttan should go. Kuttan had forgiven his mother once he realised what true love actually meant though never admitted to self. Now he could find reasons to explain even the most bizarre. So, he was here standing in front of the door of the old enormous traditional villa owned by the land lord Ramesh and his ancestors.

Kuttan had left his mother about fifteen years ago when she decided to marry Ramesh. Since then he had never visited them.

"How are you son?" asked Ramesh. Kuttan didn't respond.

"I asked, how are you Kuttan?" Ramesh repeated his question.

"Survived. Where is 'my' mother?" Kuttan responded without much consideration. He had heard the question at once but didn't approve Ramesh calling him son, so he didn't reply.

"She is in her room, second from the right. She has waited for you her whole life," Ramesh realised the displeasure of Kuttan.

"Me too," Kuttan replied staring at Ramesh and then moved towards the room.

The mother had a cancer in the small intestine which had spread to the lungs. After initial diagnosis and management three years ago, she refused for any further treatment. She wanted her life to end in pain and suffering. The pathway to *moksha* was through repentance and suffering, she believed.

He entered the dimly lit room after taking a moment of deep breath, to make sure he won't cry. The mother was lying on the old rosewood bed, unable to move; even breathing took a lot of effort on her part. She was only skin and bone. Kuttan felt terrible looking at her. Even if he hated her for letting someone else love her, he had always admired her beauty. He always loathed how she could give birth to an ugly creature like him. His feet felt weakened to take few more steps to reach her when she became aware of his presence. She looked at him from the corner of her eye. A tear drop rolled from her eye making a track over the malar.

"Kuttan! Come a bit closer son," she requested with lot of effort to raise her head.

He moved slowly towards her. With every step forward he noticed a new sign of ageing and weakness on her body. He sat on a stool kept at her bedside. He didn't say a word. He was sad. A deep melancholy pinched him inside. For the first time he felt he had let her down. He was not a good son. He didn't take care of her. He took her hand and held it tight. It was too late now, her soul was ready for departure. No one could have held her back. All she waited was to see her beloved son for one last time and then she could die in peace.

She was opening and closing her mouth as if finding it difficult to swallow her own saliva. Kuttan didn't understand.

"She needs some water. A few ounce of water from your hand may soothe her burning soul," Ramesh instructed standing at the door.

Kuttan didn't respond. He took the mother's head in his lap

and poured a few drops of water in to her mouth. Little went down the throat, most spilled out. He could not stand this anymore. His guilt was becoming unbearable. He never understood his mother. She was in love. He could realise only after he felt the love for Maya, even then he never admitted.

"How are you? I thought I won't be able to see you. I had prayed for you always, it was the only thing I could do for you," she said in blurred voice with words barely audible.

"I know Amma. I should have come earlier. But, I was not sure how to face you in your new role, what to say or how to meet your eyes?" He bent down with his lips only few centimetres away from her right ear and whispered, "I am sorry Amma, and I will miss you. I had always loved you but didn't realise it until…" he chocked and could not finish the sentence. Tears rolled out of her eyes. He sucked drop from the cheek and kissed her good bye.

He didn't turn back. He could not hold his tears. He nauseated. He ran as hard as possible out of the huge metal gate, through the plantation past the paddy fields towards his old house where they had lived happily as a family for four years, the only four years of peace and happiness they ever had.

***

He stood in front of the ruins of his old *palace* which stood in someone else's property now. No money could buy him those wonderful days when he lived at this place with his father and mother. He missed those blissful days. He had learnt the hard way that money could buy a lot of other things and gave one a sense of protection. So he invested his whole life in saving money. How foolish he was? He was yet to realise.

There was not much left of the house. The remaining four walls and pillars of the single room house was devoid of any roof. Doors and windows, which had provided feast to termites for a long time crumbled under their own weight. He stood in the middle of the reminiscent hall looking at the blue sky remembering his father.

He missed his *Uppa*.

Chapter 2

Uppa

Dileep, named by his *Amma*, was fondly called Kuttan by his father, *Uppa*. They shared a special bond; a bond which he would not have with anyone else ever for the rest of his life. Not many knew him as Kuttan. His mother used to call him by the name which he didn't appreciate. He has had many nick names in his life, most of them used by his peers to tease him. But, Kuttan remained his favourite because it was his father who called him so.

Kuttan didn't have many memories of his father. He had lost him at a very young age. But he remembers that he loved him very much. His father and mother belonged to different communities. Deeply in love, they refused to bow down to the social norms. The norms which wouldn't let them live a life of love and peace together. They challenged those norms and the people who followed them religiously.

Result? They had to leave their native place in Kasargod, Kerala and move to a small village in southern part of Kerala, Ullanoor. A place where they hoped to be away from the demons of divisions in their life, little did they know that such a place didn't exist with men around.

Ullanoor was a small yet beautiful village with paddy fields on either side of a main road which connected to the nearest town Pandalam. The raised lands were mostly used for banana, coconut and tapioca plantations. Most of the houses were small yet well maintained. But now the scenery had changed. Paddy fields were sparse. The raised lands were occupied by huge mansions and houses of NRIs; the houses which were hardly occupied on most part of the year. Banana plantations had paved way to rubber plantations. With the rubber trees coming in to the fore, the native coconut trees have *bid adieu,* almost.

The memories Kuttan had of the time were the ones which still gave him nightmares. From the main road laid a thin mud track, lined along the paddy fields, leading to their hut about two kilometres from the road. The mud track was deserted for most of its length. It was lined by dense bushes on one side and paddy fields on the other. The area was infamous for the various kinds of venomous reptiles it inhabited. They were supposed to reach home every day before sunset, without fail.

His father would carry him all along the mud track so that he could keep a vigilant eye on the track with the torch that hardly showed light few feet ahead.

That day Kuttan insisted that he would walk as he was old enough to take care of himself; how true was he? His loving father hesitantly agreed to the demand. The sun had already set and it was getting darker and darker with each step they made towards their home.

Kuttan was enjoying his freedom. He was a boy proud of his ability to explore new things at the very young age of four. Since he was walking a few feet ahead and running in between, his father had to show light in front to his child.

All of a sudden he heard his father's cry, "Kuttan! Go... run fast. Get some help. I have been bitten by a snake."

He did mention the name of snake but Kuttan couldn't recall it. He had heard of it before and knew it was something to be afraid of. He remembered how his father's face turned pale. In the dim light of torch lying down, he could see his father sweating with eyes wide open. He was struggling to stay awake. His slurred speech pleaded Kuttan to run as fast as possible and get some help.

Kuttan knew it was his mistake. Had he stayed in his father's lap this could have been avoided. He got scared. He ran as hard as he could have at the age. He went beneath the bed, the sole furniture in the house. He used to hide their, afraid of evil spirits, when his parents were not home. He would come out when they returned, and everything would become normal. He believed the bed had some magical powers. He stayed there till next day morning hoping the magical powers of the bed would save his father.

Next day morning he was awaken by his mother's screams, when the neighbours brought his father home packed in white cloth. What happened after he ran from there he was not sure. He didn't have the courage to ask anyone. His mother cried aloud cursing him for the misery he had brought to them. He watched everything from underneath the bed.

He regretted every moment of the day. He had wished so many times that he could turn back the clock and change the events. But they were not supposed to be changed. He regretfully realised that the bed didn't possess any magical powers. Fate was something that he couldn't change. He was always to be held responsible for the death of his father; less by the world, more by himself.

He performed the last rituals for his father and buried him as was told by the elders with long beard. Although his *Uppa* had chosen his mother over their religion, she was not allowed to come near his father's corpse as she had not accepted his religion. Their love was not enough to purify her to make any concessions. Along with his father's soul he performed the rituals for the soul of the boy who was an explorer by nature, who could have taken any risk without fear.

Chapter 3

Maman

Kuttan and his mother had difficult times after his father's death. They were made to sell their small house to pay back the lenders, the money that his father had owed them. Some of them were his father's 'friends'. They used to come there frequently to have food at 'their' home; he used to call them uncles.

For some strange reasons beyond young Kuttan's intelligence they didn't seem to be as friendly as they used to be. They abused his mother and one of them even had beaten her. Finally, a good man, a rich one, came for their rescue. He bought their house and land for some good amount and settled all their debts. He offered his mother a job in his coconut plantation and offered free education for her son. An offer she, helpless, could have never let go. All she cared was her son's secured future. She agreed, for everything. He loved the uncle and called him Ramesh*maman*. *'Maman'* meant uncle in his native tongue, Malayalam.

Ramesh*maman* lived in a huge mansion near the biggest coconut plantation of the village on the opposite side of the main road. He allowed them to shift to the small house within his plantation. He joked with him to be the caretaker at the plantation. That would mean he will have to sleep in veranda of the house and keep a vigil if anyone comes. It was not a joke; he was supposed to keep vigil.

Ramesh*maman* would come to their house at nights with irregular frequencies. On such nights, Kuttan had to sleep outside, in the veranda and keep vigil. While leaving *maman* would give him a two rupee note which he kept in a small empty oil tin.

Later the frequencies of the visit increased. He enquired with his mother about purpose of his visit. His mother would at times refuse to answer, at times she would slap him and other times would tell him that he was their landlord and came to settle the money matters. He was confused thinking why he was paid for keeping vigil outside when they were settling money matters, but didn't have the courage to ask any details for the fear of getting beaten up.

***

Ramesh*maman* had three children, two boys and a girl. One boy was three years elder to Kuttan, one boy was of the same age and the girl was one year younger to him. The boys were not considerate but the baby girl used to smile at him. Kuttan envied them. They had beautiful dresses, toys and played as long as they wanted. They went to school. They had all sort of vegetarian and non-vegetarian delicacies as per their wish. Kuttan wanted to play with them and be like them but was not allowed to go in to their house as he would have 'spoilt' them.

They would at times come to the plantation with their father. But, those times Ramesh*maman* would not come in to their house to discuss money matters. He didn't have the courage to ask, so he satisfied his curiosity by thinking that, *"May be money matters are better discussed in the silence of a dark night."*

He realised very early in his life that the only difference between Ramesh*maman's* children and him was that they were rich. They had money and a father to take care of their needs. He was supposed to take care of himself and make money enough to go to school and have food at least two times daily.

The promise that Ramesh*maman* made regarding his education seemed hollow as he wanted him to work in the plantation which was not acceptable to his mother. She always encouraged him to study and have a better future for him and may be herself in some distant future.

Kuttan's mother bought him a bicycle and arranged a job for him. He was six years old, old enough to earn for his needs. He had to deliver newspaper to the houses in the morning. He would start at five in the morning and delivered paper to about hundred houses by eight.

He would get one hundred rupees per month as salary. He needed only about fifteen rupees for his educational needs rest all he saved in the oil tin. His dream of beautiful dress, toys and better food he had put aside to save money as much, and as early as possible to lead a rich better life in the future.

Chapter 4

Vavachi, the first love

On way to the government primary school, where he studied, Kuttan would daily observe Ramesh*maman's* children dressed in bright neatly ironed uniforms and imported school bags waiting for their convent school bus. The bags were gifted by their relatives in the distant fairy land called Gulf. They had lots of money for the extravagant life style but he could not afford it, Kuttan reminded himself while trying to reduce the number of creases on his shirt with his tender small hands.

At school, his life was not easy either. Kuttan, at the age of six had only a built of four. His nutritionally depleted body was constantly subjected to bullying by other children. He felt that the humiliations and fights he was subjected to were not solely because of his body size but also because of the fact that he didn't have a father to be afraid of. He missed his father deeply. He could do nothing about that but he could be rich by saving lots of money, that would solve all his problems, he believed.

After school he had found a job at the tea shop nearby his school opposite to the temple. He had to stay at the hotel to serve the customers, many were his father's old friends, till closure. He would clean tables, serve water and sometimes food too when Balan, the main waiter, was too busy. The hierarchy had to be strictly followed. The owner, Bhaskaran*maman*, would give him fifty rupees per month and dinner consisting of whatever was excess on that day. It was the best and most satiable meal of the day Kuttan would have. That meant more savings for Kuttan, so he never complained.

Thanks to the revolution among workers and high literacy rates, those days the paddy fields were converted in to cricket grounds in the summer, where tournaments were held every summer vacation. Any child would have dreamed to play in the tournament but, not Kuttan. He saw it as a business opportunity, his first entrepreneurship assignment. He struck a deal with Bhaskaranmaman to sell lemon sodas and traditional tea shop snacks consisting *murku, pazham poris and vadas*. The profit was shared fifty percent between two of them. This remained a custom every summer vacation till he was there, the menu and profits kept increasing.

Bhaskaranmaman understood Kuttan's desire to earn money. He appreciated that he never tried any short cuts but preferred to work hard at young age. So, he happily agreed. Every weekend Bhaskaranmaman would reward his hard work and determination with four spherical Parle's orange candies, twenty five paise each, wrapped in transparent plastic wrap with white print on them. Kuttan would lick them slowly and intermittently so that they lasted whole week until next weekend.

One vacation the tea shop was forced to close for few days when Bhaskaran*maman* fell ill. Kuttan prayed for his health as the more number of sick days for Bhaskaran*maman* would have meant less savings and loss of delicious dinner for Kuttan. But his prayers were not heeded as usual and Bhaskaran*maman* remained sick for more than one month.

Those days Kuttan had nothing to do as he didn't have friends to play with. So he was excited to join *Vavachi*, Ramesh*maman*'s daughter, when she invited him to play with her. She was affectionately called Vavachi, for Kuttan she was dearer and hence *Vava*, the baby. She was the only lovable creature he could think of in the village other than his mother. She never made fun of his looks, his dress, him being poor, or the gap left by the departed upper front teeth.

Kuttan was supposed to obey her commands which he loved to do. He would climb trees without any fear and pluck the fruit of her choice. She too loved the way Kuttan treated her. She was special for him and Kuttan would do everything to make sure that she realised it. Their friendship didn't go down well with her brothers, but on *Vava's* insistence Ramesh*maman* allowed Kuttan to stay in the compound to play with her.

As the days were moving faster than they used to, Kuttan wished Bhaskaran*maman* to remain sick for few more days. He didn't want to feel guilty for not working hard and earning money, instead wasting time with the most loving girl in the world. His good health would have robbed Kuttan of the reason he desperately needed. But his happiness ended abruptly yet again.

One evening as usual Kuttan and Vava were playing. Kuttan was obeying her commands and in turn he received precious 'Gulf' chocolates. He heard noises coming from her house. It was very common for Ramesh*maman* and wife to argue and fight over every possible issue one could think of. But that day it was more vicious. The blows were harder and the cries louder.

From nowhere her mother charged towards him and started slapping and abusing him and his mother for ruining her life. First Kuttan stood and then he laid there until she had her fury satisfied. Her brothers joined their mother and kicked Kuttan, they had their reasons. Getting beaten for no reason was not unusual for him but this time the beating was vigorous and what hurt him the most was that neither Ramesh*maman* nor Vavachi tried to stop them. He was thrown out of the compound. Throughout the beating Kuttan made sure he didn't lose hold of his precious possession- the Gulf chocolates.

***

Kuttan's days became monotonous. His routine kept on repeating with only one change. Vava was not present anywhere around. Her mother had left Ramesh*maman* and took three of her children along with her to some unknown far place where only women and children were allowed. No men could dare to go near them as they were prohibited by serpent deities. He wanted to enquire but again he was too afraid to do so. He missed her. His first love was lost before even he could realise what he felt was love. He missed her calling him *"pottan Kuttan"* which meant stupid Kuttan. He was stupid to love her and was even more stupid to miss her at nights looking at the starry sky; he remained stupid all his life.

Only relief were the Gulf chocolates which he licked daily at night and wrapped back in to the tin. The expensive chocolates were like expensive people, they had to be used and taken care of with utmost attention, or else they could mess up things around them, some times which could mean a childhood.

The chocolate melt in his mouth blending with sound of cry of crickets at night lazily crackling without purpose. The cool breeze in the night would play its magic on him and he would sleep with a smile through the night.

Chapter 5

Marriage and Separation

As time passed Kuttan grew, with him grew his insecurities. Although his physical growth was not as much as his peers, but still he could be called an adolescent. He had joined Government higher secondary school in the town, five kilometres from his place of stay. He and his mother still lived in Ramesh*maman's* plantation. After his wife left him, Ramesh*maman's* visits to their house became more frequent. Kuttan, after the beatings and abuses he had received from Vava's mother few years back, realised that these visits were not just to discuss money matters. But he was too afraid to ask or protest. Ignorance seemed a blessing, not for long though.

"Why does Ramesh uncle visit Dileep's house so frequently brother?" asked one of his class mates to another one ignoring Kuttan's presence on purpose, surrounded by a group of little devils.

"Don't be too innocent as if you don't understand these things?" replied another boy midst to the giggles of other children.

"What things," asked another 'friend'?

"The money matters," said the first boy patting on to Kuttan's shoulder followed by a piercing laugh. Kuttan had tried to reason with him.

Kuttan had once innocently told one of the guys, who pretended to be a sympathiser, what he believed about the visits. Kuttan didn't want to believe the obvious truth. The squeeze on the shoulder and the pats on the back were painful, but more painful were the giggles. Kuttan didn't move an inch from his place. He was surrounded by boys and girls who laughed at the pitiable life he had at the mercy of Ramesh, they would not let him run away. He didn't dare fight them for fear of getting beaten up which was a usual time-pass for the bullies. He stood there helpless looking at the floor, eyes wet and filled. He missed a protective hand over his head.

"Please let me go," he exploded and ran away; the giggles and laughs didn't stop, they followed him.

In the night when Ramesh (he didn't consider him to be *maman* anymore) visited his house, Kuttan refused to let him in. He refused to leave the room and threatened to make noise.

"Leave my mother and get out of our house," shouted Kuttan at the owner of the properties.

"Why don't you wait outside son, you may earn a bit more tonight?" Ramesh didn't take the threat seriously. He pushed him aside and went in.

"I don't need your money. Get out!" shouted Kuttan.

With all his power he held Ramesh from the back trying to pull him out. Ramesh turned around and held Kuttan by his neck against the wall, choking him. Kuttan tried to push Ramesh away, out of the room. He choked, the eyes propped out, face turned blue but he didn't give up, and continued to put on a fight for the first time in his life.

The struggle resulted in shouts and cries. The mother stood perplexed. She reacted just in time and made sure that her son was not choked to death. Kuttan's act of defiance proved too much for her to stand. She cried and begged Ramesh to leave as she was ashamed and didn't want her status to deteriorate any further.

"Please Ramesh*cheta* leave. I beg you. If you can't give me the status that would get me respect in the society then please don't spoil it further," she was at Ramesh's feet.

Ramesh was upset about the humiliation he had received at

the hand of Kuttan. He left. He didn't ask Kuttan and his mother to leave the plantation. Kuttan too didn't want to leave as it would have meant additional financial burden and would have burnt in to his savings which was now a few thousand rupees. Thus, the visits stopped after the rebellion but the miseries did not.

*****

Kuttan and his mother never discussed the incidence after that night but it stayed between both of them, like weeds in unwanted lands, like an intractable thorn stuck somewhere deep, for the rest of their lives. Kuttan never cared what his mother felt. She didn't have the courage to express it. He avoided all possible circumstances that could have forced him to talk to her. She never complained. She didn't have any explanations, trustworthy enough, for him. She had her reasons which he would not have understood. He too never questioned or harassed her. He didn't have questions worth asking her. He felt betrayed.

Left alone and vulnerable, she married Ramesh. Whether they were in love or was it his revenge for the night, Kuttan didn't know, and didn't care either. She earned a husband and painful luxurious life for herself while Kuttan struggled, worked hard and saved for a distant bright future. He didn't move in to Ramesh's house. Kuttan and his mother were two strangers captive in this cruel world, strangled by their sorry lives until Maya came in to his life.

He left the house in his step-father's plantation. He moved to the tea shop. He shared the servant rooms at the tea shop with the senior waiter. He never visited them ever since then. Ramesh was the reason he had lost his only family left; he could not pardon him like he could never forgive himself for his father's death.

*****

Kuttan stood still in the ruins, eyes fixed at the afternoon sky. Sweat formed pearls on the forehead and a few drops draining along the hairline. It was usually very humid at this place. The place was dampened, so were his spirit. Then he felt few drops of rain drops hitting against his face. It was raining under the sun. A rainbow appeared on west side against the backdrop of coconut trees lining the paddy field. Children get amused by such magic of the Mother Nature. It brought a smile on his face like a balm applied over an old sore wound.

Lost in his thoughts, he was brought back to the present by some rustling of the dried leaves outside. Someone was coming towards him. He turned around, it was Ramesh standing at the entrance.

Chapter 6

The end of a painful journey

Ramesh looked at Kuttan standing at a distance from the entrance. He didn't enter the ruins of the house. His eyes looked tired. Tired from taking care of a soulless sick body for long. They needed some rest. He didn't disown his wife when she was sick and had struggled. He loved her beyond the physical needs, as was supposed by Kuttan and others. He was a caring husband. Why did he cheat on his first wife? He was human and had erred. There was no love left in their relation; they merely existed. Sometimes even two good human beings put together cannot stitch together a good relation. This was the only explanation he had for himself as no one else had ever asked what he felt.

Kuttan looked at him. Ramesh's eyes told Kuttan what his lips failed to reveal. He was relieved of his duties- a caretaker husband. The ruins of the house symbolised Kuttan's broken family, his spoilt childhood. He had done a great injustice to a mother and her son. He repented for his sin.

Ramesh stood there for some time then said, "All are waiting for you," he didn't speak a word until then.

"Hmmm," Kuttan sighed. He felt a deep ache but he was happy for his mother. *"Finally her sufferings has come to an end,"* he thought. A tear drop broke through the barricade of control and fell down getting lost in hundreds of drops around.

Lost in thoughts Kuttan followed Ramesh.

She wished to leave this world as soon as possible. The best possible solution to all the miseries was *the end,* though the manner of putting an end is important. The end seems so peaceful but then one has to suffer all the pain allotted before 'the journey' begins. For some, such is life, a cruel joke. The pain is felt only as long as one resist. Once submitted to the cause of fate, the pain and the life seem inseparable. She had accepted that she might not see her beloved son ever again before her death. Hence she was at peace during the last two, most painful, years of her life. The pain was physical, hence minimal.

The corpse was incinerated unlike his father which was buried. Then he had put soil onto the coffin now, he had to set fire beneath the wooden platform. He stood there and watched his mother melt away, turning into ashes and fumes deeply darkened. The body seemed to melt in to the soil and dark fumes were the sufferings and miseries. The smoke seemed infinite produced by a weakened finite body.

When dead, Kuttan would like the corpse to be burnt. Then the strongest fume and the darkest smoke from his burning pyre would darken the brightest sky; blackening the face of *the God* up there who never leaves His comfort, and let His creatures suffer infinitely.

Kuttan was lost in his thoughts, he didn't notice the fire had faded. Only the ashes were left, releasing smoke. Ramesh stood beside him. His wrinkled old face staring at the fumes coming out of the ashes. He stood there probably wondering what would happen to his soul. Would it wander without peace for want of anyone to perform last rituals? Maybe that would be his punishment for the sins he had committed in this life.

"There was a phone call for you," Ramesh said as he tried to hide his emotions.

"I wonder, what happens to the souls?" Kuttan asked without any preamble, eyes still fixed onto the ashes as if he knew exactly what was going in Ramesh's mind.

"Some find peace and some wander," Ramesh sighed, and answered without looking at Kuttan reflecting his thoughts.

"Why is life so complicated?"

"I don't know, may be our deeds are responsible."

"I do not agree. Some suffer for no fault of theirs. Sometimes their whole childhood is lost in the struggle," Kuttan looked at Ramesh, his eyes reddened.

"I am sorry son. It is not the way you think. I know you can never forgive me but you should know that I really loved your mother. My relation with Vavachi's mother had spoiled beyond repair long before I had met your mom. And..." Ramesh was interrupted by the gesture of Kuttan, looking away with a raised hand.

"I know it might take a lifetime for you to explain and still you won't be able convince me. It's just your guilt as you near the fag end of your life. I am not in a mind-set to listen to any of these, not now and maybe never," Kuttan didn't want to keep any grudge but to forgive Ramesh was going to take much more time and probably would had been only next to forgiving himself. He left without noticing a sobbing weak old Ramesh.

***

Kuttan had to stay back for a few more days to complete the last rituals. He didn't wish to stay in the village so, he decided to leave to Kochi and stay in an ashram. He had stayed during his undergraduate days in this ashram, volunteering himself to help in kitchen for exchange of free stay and food. He planned to come back just in time for the rituals. But before that, he wished to go to the tea shop where he had stayed and worked. He owed a lot to Bhaskaran*maman*. He would not have survived without his support. The support and care would have continued if it was not for his stupidity. But then he had no regrets as all the past incidences were taking him close to his destiny, his love Maya.

Chapter 7

The tea shop and the trunk

Kuttan was standing at the small junction of three roads in front of the primary school with two temples on either side. The smaller temple on the southern side had been renovated recently and was looking artificially elegant with shining roof tiles and copper plated lamps mounted on the side walls. The bigger temple towards the northern side was the older one. It looked dull with roof tiles darkened due to algae dried on its surface. The lamps around the temple walls were made of stones beautifully carved and mounted on to the marble walls. The lamps were lit as a preparation for *Deeparadhana*, the prayers offered to the deity with lamps at dusk. People waited patiently everyday outside the sanctum sanctorum of the temple for the doors to open with all the lamps lightened and the priest offering prayers to the goddess. Many people waited out there, Bhaskaran*maman* was one among them. Kuttan waited for him outside the tea shop looking at the people wondering what these people achieved by repeating the same routine every day.

He had worked there at the tea shop for many years but never visited either of the two temples. He never felt some one important was in there worth taking the pain of bowing and praying. He would have rather bowed to Bhaskaran*maman*, so that he might have increased his salary. He always wondered how much did the rich in his village spent on these religious activities. Had they donated the one hundredth of that for the education and upliftment of poor children, then they would also have had the opportunity to fulfil their dreams. Maybe that is what they exactly wished not to happen. Maybe these were the bribes paid to keep them rich and the poor poorer. The goddess was probably conspiring with the rich men; the poor had little to offer.

"One day I would be rich, someone important. I won't donate a single rupee to any temple or mosque, rather would build a school for poor children where they could have free education," Kuttan promised himself. He was lost in his thoughts, when the bells started ringing in the temple rhythmically, as the door of the sanctum sanctorum opened, which brought him back to the real world- a world where he had struggled a lot to make a space for himself.

"Kuttan!" Bhaskaran*maman* could not believe his eyes. His old eyes recognised him even after a long gap of time. He had heard about the demise of Kuttan's mother but was not sure if Kuttan would visit.

Kuttan responded with a smile wrapped in embarrassment generated from memories he had of the place. Thirteen years ago Kuttan had left the place shamed and beaten for engaging in adultery; to be specific, for accompanying Balan, the waiter, in his *adventure*. If it was not for an *angel thief*, he would have been doomed inside some jail or may have died at the hands of police, the moral one.

"I prayed to meet you son. I had been praying to the mother Goddess Shakti Mahamaya daily for your well-being ever since you had left this place. I was worried, how you would survive? Thank God you are safe and healthy," Bhaskaran*maman* cared for Kuttan. He was one of the few well-wishers Kuttan had in the village, probably the only one alive now.

"I too wished to come but somehow didn't have the courage. Now, when I saw my mother on death bed I realised you must have grown old too," Kuttan was not sure how to respond. His words could not convey his thoughts. He seemed overwhelmed by the memories running through the circuits in his mind, sparking a sense of shock within himself.

"You must have thought next time this old man might not be around. So, you came to visit me one last time before it was too late," Bhaskaran*maman* laughed aloud making fun of Kuttan, exposing dark shadow of his upper lips and grey moustache on to the discoloured spaced front teeth. He patted on Kuttan's back and led him in to the tea shop.

After tea with Bhaskaran*maman*, Kuttan climbed over clankingly crying old wooden stairs to reach his old room filled by old junk and inhabited by rodents. At the right corner, he saw the old trunk that he had left, unmoved. Bhaskaran*maman* had left it untouched, he might have expected Kuttan to come back.

In the hurry that night, he had managed to take along with him only the few thousand rupees he had saved through his childhood and the small trunk that was not too heavy to carry and run. Still the memory of that night haunted Kuttan.

Chapter 8

Secretive adventure with a despicable friend

Kuttan stayed at the tea shop for three years after his mother got married to Ramesh. Meanwhile, Kuttan limped through his schooling days. He passed the board examination with second class. It didn't matter as he never cared if anything better was available. He believed one cannot become rich by just studying hard and getting first class marks. Schools were only manufacturing workers and slaves for multinational corporate houses. They were not promoting free thinkers and entrepreneurs. He wished to become a business man, an entrepreneur, a job giver rather than a job seeker.

One of the few things that attracted Kuttan during his school days was computer. When he was in ninth standard, a computer lab started in his school. *"It is the future, a wonder machine that would run the whole world. So better get used to it, earlier the better,"* they were told by the computer teacher in the introductory class. He also named a few eminent Indians who were doing big business in the computer world.

Most of the school education had vaporized but the introductory computer class and one particular south Indian name stuck within his head. He had read about the person in a Sunday supplement of

Malayala Manorama newspaper while he was packing *pazham poris* with it. He too dreamt of going to a big city and make a name of his own but never dared to discuss it with anyone for the fear of being ridiculed. He wished to start an IT firm of his own and churn out huge money, like *"the famous rich from rags"* success story he had read in the newspaper. He wished to metamorphose from a ragamuffin in to a rich entrepreneur.

Kuttan had thought of starting a small computer business with his savings. But he had no idea about doing a modern day business, his only experience was selling snacks and lemonade at the cricket ground, which was small yet profitable. The thought of risking all his life time savings in to a single venture made him nervous. Though the saving was small, it provided him with a sense of protection which made him wary of parting with it. He dreamed big but lacked a heart to match it. He decided to play safe.

Kuttan was confused whether to join college or earn more money to start a business. He found a midway. He decided to work at the tea shop as full time waiter for two years at a salary of four thousand per month and then he would join BSc computer science course. He would learn about the computers and business, and then definitely he will start the business, he promised self. He decided to delay the obvious; he knew he would have to take risk at some point of time, he will have to part away with his savings. He was not ready, not yet.

***

The *senior* waiter, Balan, was twenty five years of age, and was there at the tea shop for the past ten years. He earned two hundred rupees daily. He would spend the money on anything that gave him pleasure. To dream big, to save and be rich, live an ethical and moral life, such thoughts never existed for him. If Kuttan was ever to become a phenomenon then Balan would have been the antonym.

Kuttan had to share the room with Balan. Balan slept on the bed while Kuttan had to sleep on the floor. Balan had always envied Kuttan for studying while working and thus earning the money and respect from the people around. He tried many times to make Kuttan spend the money like he did, but in vain. Kuttan didn't like his company, but he still preferred to stay with him as none of his old schoolmates dared to mess with Balan for the kind of rowdy reputation he had. Balan never teased Kuttan for his past which was a reason good enough to be with him. Thus, he had a *'friend'* finally, a despicable one.

Kuttan was Balan's key to achieve social acceptance and respect. Hence he would ask Kuttan to join him wherever he went during free time, at times in the nights for his *adventures*, as a cover. And the result? Kuttan lost his grace and credibility, whatever little he had earned.

Balan had many *pleasurable, adventurous* activities like making and selling illicit liquor, gambling, going to prostitutes and most pleasurable was infidelity; having affair with married women whose husbands were in gulf countries for work. He preferred air-conditioned bungalows with soft foam beds. He loved the idea of having sex with the women of rich 'bastards' in the comfort of their bed rooms. It was his way of avenging an unjust society that left him poor and turned him in to a thug. Although it never mattered, but Kuttan didn't agree with him.

***

That day, when his peers teased Kuttan, he came running back to home. He didn't go to the tea shop. His ears were filled with the laughs of the little devils. The taunt chased him, "Don't be too innocent as if you don't understand these things?" What were 'those' things? Even when Kuttan pretended ignorant, he knew those were not money matters but wanted to know what exactly happened behind the closed doors of his house once Ramesh went inside.

Once the door was closed, he could hear the giggles and laughs from the inside which later turned in to moans. Earlier Kuttan never dared to look inside. He was afraid of discovering the truth. On that night, Kuttan peeped in through the gap in the window panel. He was not shocked. But was pained at the thought that the only person, he believed, he had perhaps didn't belong to him anymore.

He saw his mother in arms with Ramesh. Both of them would

laugh at him. The laughs would turn in to moans and again laughter. The group of little devils would join the chorus. They would chase him to the end of a cliff. He had jumped of the cliff numerous times but never managed to reach the bottom so as to put an end to his miseries. He would wake up panting in to the darkness of night which seemed lighter when compared to the black hole within him.

He had had many such nightmares since the incidence.

***

Kuttan followed Balan under the moonlight aiming for a mansion next to the church at the end of mud track along the paddy field. The mud tracks lead to the rear gate of the bungalow. The front main road was avoided as many houses were lined along the road. The paddy fields were deserted and no one used these tracks other than *adventurous* people, for these were dreaded for inhabiting poisonous reptiles. No one knew this better than Kuttan; still he wished to walk on the track without a torch. But the destiny doesn't heed to one's wish, it seems to have other plans, always.

The bluish moonlight was hindered by a huge tree and dense vegetation in the backyard of the house. They incised through the darkness to reach the back door. Balan knocked at the door in rhythmic manner of 'three...two...one' three times. Kuttan had heard this rhythmic code of Balan before.

"If he had used this brain for any other good purpose; God knows, where he would have reached?" Kuttan thought looking at Balan meticulously executing the plan. But, Balan had reached where he wished to. The door opened after few minutes. In his front Kuttan saw a wheat complexioned middle aged woman who looked much younger. The innocence on her face was as deceptive as the intentions in her big beautiful mysterious eyes. The wet dripping untied hair filled the air with the fragrance of jasmine. It felt so nice to smell her. Before Kuttan could think any more, she frowned and asked Balan, "Who is this idiot with you? I have told you so many times don't bring any of your useless friends."

"Don't worry. He is harmless and very useful. He will keep a vigil, he is good at it. He is like a loyal puppy," Balan replied patting on

Kuttan's head and then burst in to laughter.

"Shhh... not so loud you brainless creature," she put her hand over Balan's mouth.

Balan didn't mean to hurt Kuttan, but the certification of his vigilance capabilities had churned the painful old memories that he was trying to get rid of. Kuttan again was lost in his thoughts when he heard them teasing each other playfully.

"Not so fast, you animal!" She pushed Balan aside who was trying to be too aggressive.

"You can't escape, the animal is going to tear you apart, ghrrr..." Balan jumped on to her but she ducked out.

"The prey is dying to be torn apart. But first you have to catch it," she challenged him and ran in to one of the rooms in the ground floor.

They were lost in their world and seemed totally unaware of the presence of a third soul. But Kuttan was not unaware of what was to follow, the shamelessness was too much for him to handle, so he interrupted.

"Are you married?" Kuttan asked the woman. He was very good at deception by acting fool. But, the disregard for the mood they were in was evident on his face.

She didn't respond, instead gave a stern look to Balan who jumped in to her rescue, "Mind your business child. Go stand out and look for any sign of trouble. If you stay back and poke in your nose in our personal matters you will end up in huge trouble," Balan held Kuttan by his hand and pushed him outside the house in to the back-yard. Kuttan fell down and when he looked up; he would never for-get how she looked at him with a cunning smile. She was glad at the ill- treatment of Kuttan by Balan. She was proud that her beauty had mesmerised Balan so that he chose her over his *friend*. The most perilous aspect of a beauty is when she realises how beautiful she is.

Kuttan stood outside looking at the weird patterns the clouds were making around the moon. He had seen such patterns on nu-merous occasions when he had vigilated outside his small house during his childhood. He tried to imagine various shapes in them, his favourite was that of a boat which sailed through the sky in to some unknown darkness to be never seen again. He had wished to board one such boat so many times. Being lost in the imaginary world was a luxurious bliss when the real world had nothing but struggle to offer. *"Why all these struggles? Why life was so simple for some and so complicated for others?"* he had asked himself on numerous occasions when he was a child. Failed to satisfy his queries and with no one to answer around, he buried the questions deep within himself.

He was again brought back to the reality by the giggles interspersed with moans that came from inside. Kuttan felt terrible standing outside cursing his fate. When the self-pity became unbearable he went inside, he was about to knock the door when he again heard the moans. Instead of knocking at the door he ended up peeping through the door which was not latched from inside.

She was covered by a blanket up to her waist with bosoms exposed. The dresses they worn were lying at the floor. Balan was not seen, but a hump kept moving within the blanket which made her moan even more. She cried and shouted in between. At times she pleaded to stop while at other times she commanded him. The 'vulgarity' of the scene was unbearable. He stormed in to the room and pulled the naked woman out of her bed. Before they could understand anything Kuttan slapped her twice, "Have some shame you whore, you horny bitch!"

When Balan realised what had struck them he jumped out of the bed and kicked Kuttan down on to the floor. Kuttan tried to retaliate but he was too strong for him and soon was joined by the woman. They kicked Kuttan again and again. Kuttan didn't give up, he fought back. Kuttan managed to get hold of her legs and pulled her down, her head struck against the corner of the bed and started bleeding. At the sight of blood Balan panicked. It gave Kuttan the time stand up on his feet. They exchanged few more blows. The shouts and cries increased with the fury. Kuttan was beaten badly but he managed inflict injuries to both. His own clothes were torn. They were two and half naked scattered in the room with bloodied floor, which resembled a crime scene. The resultant noises attracted the neighbours and passer-by. The *secretive adventure* was not a secret anymore.

Chapter 9

An angel thief

The people who had gathered in the house were shocked to see the poor woman lying naked at the floor in a pool of blood. She was bleeding from her head and private parts. Poor soul was attacked by two animals; criminal bastards. Thank God! The vigilant neighbours reached in time or else the poor soul would have suffered at the hands of immoral thugs.

"How can a woman be safe in a country where such devils existed?" No questions were asked; there was no need to. Everything seemed as clear as broad daylight under the moon.

How could such a beauty lie? She declared to the judicious mob that she was robbed and raped by these two heartless men. Balan tried to protest and resist while Kuttan held his head down. He wished them to beat him dead. But how could a civilised, cent percentage literate society have killed anyone; so they stripped him, and tied them naked to the huge tree in the backyard.

Police was informed who said they were busy with another raid somewhere else. Moreover, when told that the culprits were caught red handed and tied to a tree, they *knew* that they didn't have much to worry. They informed the responsible mob to leave them as such and warned them against disturbing the crime scene. The poor woman was rushed to a nearby hospital. The mob satisfied at the fulfilment of their social responsibility left the place with Balan and Kuttan helpless and tied to the tree with different ropes.

***

Balan was crying like a puppy who had been hit by a stone. "How could she do this to me? How can she cheat me?" he repeated every second minute.

"In the same manner as you both were cheating her husband," Kuttan carefully chose words that could lacerate Balan's already wounded heart.

"You idiot! Tell me how can we get out of it?" Balan was getting desperate.

"No way out of here Mr Arse. We are screwed," Kuttan had accepted the fate. They were to be tried for rape and attempted robbery, and hopefully hanged.

"Kuttan! Please tell the police that you had an affair with her and I had just accompanied you. I have helped you on so many occasions. You owe me so much," Balan could not stop crying.

"Haha... You are such a loser. You pussy! The police will conduct a medical examination and know who had fucked whom. I will be left with a robbery charge which never happened. So the way I look at it, I am safe and you will be screwed. Have heard that the police stabs in a tooth pick dipped in chilli powder into the penis of rape accused. May the devil bless you Balan...you bastard," Kuttan was enjoying Balan's state, though he knew his fate was no different. He looked at open sky looking at the patterns of clouds. He knew that he was going to be behind bars for some time and hence won't be able to see them soon; the realisation made the sky, the moon, stars and the cloud patterns look much more beautiful. He ceased to resist, hence there was no pain unlike Balan who kept crying. After sometime, exhausted they both fell asleep.

***

Late in that night, Kuttan woke up to some noise behind the fence of the bungalow. Someone had climbed the fence and entered the backyard. Kuttan felt a shock of fear pass through his toes via stomach. Someone had decided to rob the house in real and put the blame on them, or even worse, some of *the beauty's* 'true' lovers might have decided to do justice. A sense of doom prevailed over him. He prayed for this to be a hallucination.

He saw a figure painted black, shining with reddened eyes and sharp yellowish white teeth as it approached him. When Kuttan had cursed Balan in the name of devil, he didn't mean it. All he wished was to rub some salt on his open wounds. But, it seemed the devil didn't take it lightly.

Kuttan wanted to scream but his throat dried up. He could not even make a whisper to let Balan know about what was coming. Kuttan stared at the figure inching close to him along the thick vegetation. It reached so close that Kuttan felt his panting breath on his feet. When the figure stood straight it was only as tall and moderately built as Kuttan was. It looked straight in to his eyes, they neither carried fury nor any compassion in them, looked more human, and they seemed blank not willing to reveal the intention.

The figure took out a sharp long knife from his undergarment, the only cloth piece on his painted body. He pressed the tip against the chest of the frightened soul and moved it down taking care not to bleed him. When he reached the waist he stopped for a moment. He seemed to be casting a spell on Kuttan before he carried out the *justice*. Kuttan thought, he knew what was to follow. The *'devil thief'* was inspired by *gulf justice system*, much discussed in the state, where the rape victims were publicly killed. Was he going to chop of his penis off and bleed him to death?

"I didn't do it. He is the culprit. Please don't… " Kuttan managed to speak in a weak trembling voice, but it was too late.

'Whoosh!' sounded the blade incising through the air and passed through the rope tied around him.

Kuttan was set free by the *angel thief.* He ran for his life and never looked back. Kuttan reached the tea shop; dressed and took the money from the trunk and ran out of the village; as fast as possible, as far as possible. What happened later that night, Kuttan didn't know and never dared to enquire either?

***

'*Bang...*' the door closed behind Kuttan. He felt enfeebled by the memories; his feet seemed not to support his own body weight. He was struggling to get up from the floor when he saw a knife, an old rusted one, like the one he had seen in the hands of the *angel thief* that night. His eyes burst in to tears.

Kuttan went down to Bhaskaran*maman* with the old blade in his hand. He could not think of asking Bhaskaran*maman* anything, he hugged him tight. Bhaskaran*maman* smiled and took the knife from him, "This old blade might not be of much help anymore."

Kuttan hugged Bhaskaran*maman* tightly again and said, "Thank you."

"I am not the person whom you should thank. Hmm... but then, some things are better left unknown," the last part he said to himself looking into the sky.

Kuttan didn't hear that, he ran after a bus going to the town that was about to move from the bus stop in front of the north temple waving hand, "Wait! One person wishes to board."

***

Chapter 10

The Swami Ashram

onstant chants of recorded *'Om'* filled the air making the pleasant ashram calmer. Kuttan was sixteen kilometres away from the noises of Cochin, standing outside the gate of the 'Swami Ashram'. The ashram was abode of fifty swamis and volunteers of about the same number. It had saints of all ages but most of them were in their late sixties.

As he entered the ashram the chant became louder and clearer. At the center of the ashram stood a huge Banyan tree with a round cemented platform around painted in brick red and white borders. It was the place where the chief saint would take spiritual classes for his fellow members. All the members had to work at the ashram according to their capabilities and field of interest. Other than that they worked outside the ashram at private firms and some even in government offices to earn money and support themselves and the fellow beings; the ashram was devoid of parasites.

The ashram was spread over an area of five acres of land. It resembled more to a noble farm than a typical ashram. Here, to work and perform one's duty was believed to be the best form of devotion. Right to the banyan tree was a small temple devoted to no particular God but an almighty whom no one could see but only realise by performing his duties honestly. The bliss of self-realisation could be found only by dedication for the cause- one's duty towards the humanity and the never ending, ever changing universe. These were the few teachings of the chief saint that Kuttan remembered. One more teaching he remembered but pretended not to be aware of was that the biggest strength of a man was his belief in the *self* and biggest weakness was the greed to have more than what he deserved.

The dormitories were to the left where all the saints and volunteers rested together. Only the chief saint had a separate hut cum office. Around the place of stay was a beautiful small garden with great variety of flowering plants. The far end was lined by stables which had many kinds of dairy animals. Rest of the land was used for agriculture purpose.

It was nine in the morning when Kuttan had reached there. Most of the swamis and volunteers had gone for work after finishing their routine prayers and meditation. The chief saint, Swami Satchitananda, was watering flowers in the garden. At the sight of Kuttan, he came up to him. He carried the calmness of a wise man who had attained self-realisation; bliss he wished to help his fellow beings to know, and realize their true purpose in life. He wished Kuttan with a traditional 'Namaste' and invited him to his office room. Kuttan bowed and followed the Swami.

"Dileep! Yes, I remember you," the chief saint responded when Kuttan introduced himself formally. "How are you son? It's been long since heard anything about you."

"I am good swami*ji*. Presently, I am in Bengaluru, have been there for past few years," Kuttan replied politely.

"Oh that's good to hear. What are you doing there?"

"I am working in an IT firm there. I hope to start my own small start-up soon in partnership with my girlfriend," Kuttan replied adding the additional information on purpose. Kuttan wanted the swami to know that he was soon to become a businessman and was having a robust love life as well.

"That's wonderful Dileep. So happy for you son. You have carved your way up there. I am proud of you. I still tell the student volunteers here about your dedication and workmanship. May God bless you with all the happiness in life," Satchitananda swami didn't disappoint Kuttan then added, "But never forget the path that had leaded you up there to the happiness. That will help you regain it, if lost."

"Will never swami*ji*," Kuttan was not sure if that was a blessing or a fore-warning.

"I still remember the morning when you reached this ashram. You were so weak and terrified," swami*ji* recollected.

"I am thankful to you for supporting me through my most difficult phase,"

"Were the earlier phases easy?" Swami*ji* asked with a smile. He knew the answer.

Kuttan didn't respond with a word but just a shake of head gazing down at the table.

"Life is never meant to be easy son. It's your attitude towards the life that makes all the difference. I am just an instrument of His choice, the one who decides what help one deserves. But one thing I can assure you is that every helping hand that came your way was earned by you. You never gave up and kept fighting. He helps only those who help themselves."

The chief saint was proud of Kuttan and wished to remind Kuttan about his capabilities, the capabilities that even Kuttan was not aware of. Kuttan was not sure about 'His help being earned by him' but he managed to keep a smiling face as he bowed and paid respect to the chief saint before asking leave. There was no denial that his better days started at this place which later turned into the most wonderful ones before turning horrible again.

On his way out, Kuttan saw a kerosene lantern at the corner of the room. He felt nostalgic, "Do you still use this lantern swamiji; the world has reached much far ahead?"

"Just remember what I told you a little while back; never forget the path that leads you to the happiness."

Kuttan didn't understand what kind of response was that. What did he mean? But didn't feel like seeking any clarification. So, he smiled and moved out of the office in to the lawn of the ashram.

Chapter 11

A Call from the Past

Kuttan moved through the lawn towards the banyan tree, to the right of him was the stable for the cattle. He had fed them daily when he was there. It was part of his duty at the ashram. The other duty he was assigned with was to help the main cook with vegetables and dishes. Later, with his dedication and performance, he was promoted as assistant cook. It was during these days when he learnt the art of cooking delicious *satwik* vegetarian food.

In no time Kuttan became chief cook, Vishnudas's favourite. He taught him his secrets which he had not let anyone know thus far. It was Vishnu who insisted that Kuttan should study further and get a degree. He discussed the subject with swami Satchitanand, who was more than willing, to help him get an admission for B.Sc. computer science course at the St. Jude's college in Kochi.

It was in this college Kuttan had met Gowri whom he admired, in fact desired, to be left heartbroken later by her apathy; he believed so. Anything that would remind him about the college would in turn remind him of the sweet and sour relationship he had with her. So he preferred to keep away from the college, even though he was less than an hour away from the college.

He was roaming through the gardens of the ashram walking

down the memory lanes. Phone rang. He hurriedly took the phone out of his pocket and put it on silent mode. The call was not important, he rejected the call. Phones had to be strictly put on silent mode inside the ashram. Being away from the ashram he had forgot the rules. Moreover, he was not the terrified and weak boy anymore. He was a confident young man ready to defy the world rules; confidence that he derived from the woman in his life, Maya. How confident he was about the derived confidence was a question only a testing time could have answered. His phone again vibrated in his shirt pocket, he took the phone out irritated at being disturbed in this nostalgic moment. Didn't matter how much he denied but he still cherish his college day memories, and the time spent with Gowri.

It was Gowri calling. He was surprised by the call as they had not spoken for about one year. She had called just when he thought of her. He frowned and then hesitantly attended the phone with a deep sigh to control his anxiety and suppress any hint of excitement.

"Hello!" he hesitated.

"Hi Dileep! It's me Gowri," the voice on the other side was upbeat.

"How can girls pretend so well as if nothing was wrong even after a long break in a relationship, as he believed or just friendship, as she pretended?" Kuttan was not expecting her to converse without any hesitation.

"Hello, you there?"

"Yes Gowri. It's been long since heard anything from you. Is there anything I can do for you?" Kuttan tried to be as formal as possible.

"Anything you could do for me? You must be joking. You always needed my help Mr. Poor Guy. I used to bail you out of troubles," Gowri laughed, she didn't believe in formalities.

"You used to get me into them. Don't you remember?" Kuttan tried to counter which she ignored and continued.

"Met your friend Maya last weekend. We talked about you. So, just felt like speaking to you."

"Oh! You met her. What did she say?" Kuttan spoke in a hurried manner. He wanted to know if Maya had told her anything about their plan.

"Nothing important. Just usual talks."

"Where are you? We should meet sometime. It had been so long since we met," Gowri sounded genuine. She was always genuine. It was Kuttan who desired more from her and when he understood that he can't have her in his life as he wished, he distanced himself. Being with Maya helped. But deep inside he knew that she had never taken any advantage of him, rather she truly cared for him.

"I am in Kerala."

"What? You are in Kerala?"

"Yes. My mother expired last week. I stayed back for the funeral rites," Kuttan felt the pain at the realisation of being an orphan. Although he had always lived like an orphan, but in truth was not an orphan until last week. The absence of anyone to bless him and pray for him silently made him an orphan.

"Oh, I am so sorry. I didn't know. Maya didn't tell me either. Is there anything I could do for you?" Gowri still understood the subtle variations in his voice.

"Thanks for calling Gowri. Actually, I was thinking of you. I am at the Swami Ashram near Kochi," Kuttan was tired of pretending not excited to hear from her. The fact that she understood the change in his voice made him reveal. It was also supplemented by the fact that Maya had not called him since he left Bengaluru last week.

"Oh wow! You are there. I miss those days. They were the best in my life. So, you are going to visit our college. Lucky you; I feel jealous," the memories of those days made her joyful.

"I am not sure. I have not planned anything," Kuttan replied.

"You must be kidding. You are so nearby. You must go," Gowri almost ordered him the way she used to during college days. She could always persuade Kuttan to do what she wanted him to do. Kuttan knew that.

"I will try. I have to go now. Swami*ji* is coming, phones are not allowed here, as you know."

"How would I know? Women are not allowed in your ashram,"

Gowri teased him. She has had been there before. "And don't lie, I know no one is coming. You are just running away from the conversation. You are still that little frightened boy," Gowri laughed making fun of him.

"No, I am not lying. Have to go. Bye," Kuttan was embarrassed.

"Hmmm. Bye," she again giggled. Kuttan loved it in the past, when she teased and made fun of him. But now, Kuttan could not stand it, so he hung the phone.

Talking with her near the stable where he had first kissed her, or rather she had kissed him made Kuttan smile shyly which he wiped off his face as soon as he realised. She was such a courageous loving girl. Kuttan thought that he had left her somewhere behind in the past but a phone call from her was all needed to bring her back into his life. A sense of regret and loss crept into him. He decided to go visit his college before going back to his village the next day.

Chapter 12

Making of a Rebel

In college, Gowri had a rebellion image, but not always was she a rebel. Up to the fifth standard she lived with her par ents in Dubai. She was a happy girl with great sense of humour and wittiness which her father admired. She was a good and obedient daughter. She had a wonderful life with her parents and younger brother whom she loved deeply. But things changed when the American company where her father worked, fired him from job. The financial condition of the family became unstable; her parents decided that she along with her younger brother should live with their *Ammamma*, mother's mother, at Palakkad in Kerala until better days came.

Following years were filled with financially better emotionally worse days. Father got a better job after couple of years of struggle but children were not brought back to live with the parents as it would have affected their higher studies. They could afford only capitation fees of only one child. So, it was decided that Gowri, a doctor 'material' (according to her parents), was supposed to study for ten hours daily and crack the medical entrance exam. Her grandmother was given all the powers to make sure that she did exactly what was expected of her. What she wished and believed was not important. Her brother being not good in studies was not pushed.

Actually, he was never pushed, tested or tried in life ever. He had purposefully developed a 'good for nothing' image to help him get things done at her expense. After initial years of complaining Gowri stopped the pursuit of correcting him. Moreover, she believed that she was duty bound, being a loving daughter, to live up to her father's expectation.

At times, being a conventional duffer turned out to be a blessing. People, especially parents, would not expect anything from you. You were free to roam around, make friends, play with them, jump in to ponds and canals, get dirty, talk dirty and be dirty. Being irresponsible was acceptable. No one really cared. Someone else was working hard to make your future bright. But unfortunately, if you were tagged with a brain residing in your skull, then it would be hell out of a childhood. You were not supposed to waste time talking to friends after school. You would attend tuitions for three hours after eight hours of school. Then study for most of the remaining hours. Watching television was a privilege only duffers could have. Even having a friendly loose talk with the family might be forbidden.

One glass of *badam* milk daily was available for both, it didn't matter if you were a genius or an idiot. Being a boy was a privilege which attracted all the concessions and rewards. Boys would take care of their parents. The girl no matter however educated would be married to someone who, by the virtue of being husband, would then dictate the rest of the course of her life. Investing too much on a girl would be bad business. Moreover, if she was good at studies make her a doctor. Doctors have great value in marriage marketing. Being a doctor meant good marriage alliances. Being an NRI would not help either, NRIs ought to pay higher dowries. With so many calculations, parenting may need auditing by chartered accountants in future.

Gowri studied hard for six years, two years of entrance coaching included, but she could not crack the exam. She had disappointed her parents as she had spoiled their calculations and plans. She was dejected but that was not a problem at the house. The effort and hard work had no value without a result to show at par with the expectations.

Gowri's parents reached home to discuss future course of action. They felt betrayed, but her grandmother was not disappointed, she was judgmental as she had always been. When they were talking about her future in the front open sitting area of the old house, the grandmother told them that she always knew that Gowri was not a doctor 'material'. She didn't have the kind of dedication and focus that was needed to crack such competitive exams, she had proclaimed. According to her, it was rare to find such talents in girls, boys were more suitable for that. Actually, boys were more suitable for anything and everything.

Gowri was sitting in the room next to the sitting area. She heard everything they discussed, and felt disgusted.

"Then, why on earth did you make me invest my precious time for coaching, if you already knew that I was not a doctor material. A material? Really, is this what I am for you? I am a girl dammit! A living being. Your daughter, who sacrificed her whole childhood to live up to your expectations to end up realise that you people never believed in what you said. You liars! You gambled with my childhood and just guess who lost? Is my life a joke for you all to play with? Enough of living up to expectations of others. From here on, Gowri shall fulfil only her dreams and expectations,"

Overwhelmed with the sense of anger and disappointment, Gowri stormed in to the sitting area.

"I wish to join for BSc computer science course in Ernakulam," Gowri demanded, for the first time.

"What scope does it have?" asked her father.

"Doesn't matter? It won't cost you much. Not even one- third of the capitation fee that you are planning to spend for your son's engineering admission," Gowri had a harsh cold tone.

"Talk properly to your father," grandmother interrupted. A girl who talks back to elders would have had a terrible married life.

"When everything around you is empty, the sound resonates," Gowri was not afraid. She had invested more than what she could have in to the role of Gowri, the ideal daughter. Now it was time to invest in Gowri, the girl who wished to live her life at her own terms.

"Ok. Let it be so," her mother finalised before any further discussion could spoil the artificially cordial atmosphere at her home. She knew where Gowri was trying to take the conversation to. To accept that they had let down their child was the last thing any educated middle class parent wished to face.

Gowri didn't complain, she got what she wanted without any fuss or hard work. All that was needed was a bit of guts and openness mixed with flavours of rudeness. For the first time she had realised the power of speaking out her mind and letting people know how she felt. She had never done that before, had she realised this earlier, her childhood may not have been spoilt. But gone by was gone, she decided not to waste even a single more moment of her life for the sake of others' dreams.

"I am what I am; accept it or leave?" she reinforced the decision in her mind as she looked out of the window of her room on to the fields.

The evening sun setting down behind the faraway huge rock turned the horizon yellow-orange. For the first time in these many years the wind was soothing, it calmed her down. The paddies danced rhythmically to the tunes of chirping birds returning home after their flight of freedom. Gowri had lived there for so many years but never realised the evenings were so beautiful. She had discovered something new then; she discovered herself.

Chapter 13

The first day at college

Kuttan was standing at the front gate of the college. An unapologetic careless pack of students pushed their way past him. It was quarter past eight in the morning. Kuttan had to finish his morning duties at the ashram earlier than usual as he didn't want to be late for his first day at the college. He had got admission for BSc computer science at St. Jude's college in Kochi.

The chief saint referred Kuttan to the principal of the college who readily agreed to let him join with concessions provided to the meritorious students. Kuttan had to pay only the fifty percentages of the tuition fees.

The savings Kuttan had were only sufficient for paying fee for one or may be two years. So he had to work after four in the evening at an internet and DTP centre till nine at night. He hoped to learn more about computer business there while earning money to continue his studies. He did learn many things there but not of the kind he had expected.

Half past eight was the last bus to the ashram that helped him reach ashram just before the compulsory night prayers. Thus, the blueprint for the next three years was ready for implementation which had six hours of college, five hours of paid job, four hours of non-paid duty, two hours of travel, two hours of 'necessary for free stay' prayers and five hours of sleep and personal time.

***

"You can sit here. I don't have any problem," Gowri offered a seat beside her.

Kuttan felt out-cast at the college where the adolescents and the young adults competed to show their riches and beauty. Kuttan lacked both. The honesty and hard work that he had were the virtues of the down-cast and underprivileged.

Kuttan looked at her for a few seconds and walked past her; he saw a little plump fair girl with broad eyes who invited him to sit beside her. He didn't dare to look into her eyes again. How could a girl offer a seat to stranger; that too a boy, an uncouth one? He was puzzled. He took a seat at the back right corner where he hoped to hide from the judging curious eyes. He was so wrong.

In the first class when the professor asked everyone to introduce themselves to the class, he started from the right back corner. Kuttan stood and stared down at the slippers that he wore to the class.

"Please tell the class who you are, where you are from, what do your parents do?"

"*I am Kuttan. One of the biggest losers you may ever find. I am from Ullanoor, a sucking place in south Kerala. My father was a poor man whom I had killed. My mother is the most selfish and opportunist creature to have ever walked on the earth,*" Kuttan had his answers ready but he stood dumbfound for lack of confidence to speak in English. With all the curious eyes fixed on to him he had nowhere to escape. The sweat and shivers made him look even more ridiculous.

"Make it fast young man! We don't have all day or shall I write down the questions on board?" Professor repeated as he ran out of patience.

"Can I talk Malayalam?" Kuttan spoke his hard thought sentence only to be ridiculed further by the teacher and students alike except one. Gowri looked at Kuttan with compassion.

"No! All are supposed to speak in English in my class. If you won't speak, how will you learn?" Professor Krishna Kumar was a stubborn man.

"I am Dileep. My place Ullanoor. Father and mother dead," anyone would have cried but not Kuttan, to be mocked and ridiculed was as normal in his life as was sleeping at night. The later part made the class look away from him. Some felt sorry, some were indifferent but only Gowri still looked at him. The compassion had swollen.

"Okay. Next one please. Be fast we have already lost too much time," Professor ordered.

***

"Hi! I am Gowri," Gowri blocked Kuttan when he tried to escape from the scary place as soon as the class got over. Kuttan looked at her as if pleading to let him go. As he was about to push her aside she said, "You can speak to me in Malayalam."

"Please let me go," Kuttan tried to slide past her.

"Tomorrow you can sit with me. I promise, won't bite you," Gowri giggled at her own joke while Kuttan pushed her to move swiftly past and then through the door.

Gowri had just one reason to be friend with Kuttan, her heart wished so.

On his way out Kuttan was relieved on two accounts- firstly, the first day at college was over and second, someone beautiful in his class had spoken to him. She seemed a bit crazy to him but he appreciated that she was a considerate human.

Chapter 14

Dear looser friend

Next morning all it took was an authoritative glance from Gowri to make Kuttan sit beside her. He wished to sit with her but lacked the courage to make a move, so her glance gave him the excuse. Whole day passed but Kuttan didn't speak a word. Gowri understood that Kuttan was not comfortable among the city youngsters, and was feeling outcast. So, Gowri kept on talking despite Kuttan's seemed apathy. At the end of the day when Kuttan was about to rush to his evening job, Gowri asked him to wait for her. To his own surprise Kuttan waited. It was first time ever in his life that anyone was taking any authority over him; he missed being a child loved and cared for. Gowri understood how it felt to be left disappointed by loved ones.

"Where do you rush to, after the class?" Gowri enquired.

"I work at a DTP centre near Kaloor bus stand; have to reach there at four," Kuttan could speak to her when they were out of class. The inhibition of judging eyes didn't exist between them outside the classroom.

"You work after class. Wow! That's so cool. I wish I could be so independent someday."

"And I wish I could depend on someone someday," Kuttan said to himself with a smile, the melancholy in the eyes deceived him.

"May I ask you something? Why do you seem so sad and terrified all the time?" Gowri was looking in to his eyes.

"Don't know. May be my past experiences, I guess or maybe you have misjudged me," Kuttan looked away. After a pause he dared to look in to the eyes of Gowri and asked, "Why do you pretend to be super-happy and hyper-excited always?"

"My life experiences, I guess too," now Gowri could not meet his eyes.

There was a silence for some time. Kuttan and Gowri walked side by side with a one foot distance among them. After a few more minutes of silence Kuttan said, "I have to go now. I am already late. See you tomorrow."

"Let me think if I wish to see you?" Gowri replied with a smile. The ruth in her eyes deceived her.

Kuttan was late for job for the first time ever and he was not sorry about that. Thereafter he had been late on many occasions being equally or more unapologetic every time. He had been shy and formal with the whole world but not with Gowri. He bunked many classes with her. Walked many a miles with her. Opened his heart to her. They shared their stories with each other; their version of the story that no one bothered to listen. They shared them over many ice creams (bills were paid by Gowri).

How strange were the ways of life? When they were surrounded by many people, who were supposed to be theirs, they felt lonely. In a strange city filled with strangers they felt at home. Sometimes in life, all one need is that one person who listened to what you had to say without being judgmental; just to understand you, and not to respond. That person for Kuttan was Gowri and for Gowri that person was an illusion, a mirage in the shape and form of Kuttan.

***

One day they were having ice cream at her favourite Baskin and Robbins's when Gowri asked Kuttan to pay the bill. She had forgotten her purse in the locker. On purpose? Kuttan was not prepared for such a surprise. He was not expecting this. He had taken for granted that Gowri would do everything to make him happy without expecting anything back. Kuttan had no option but to pay the bill. The guilt of spending two hundred rupees for ice creams was too much for him to bear.

"I don't have anyone to take care of my needs unlike you. I will have to take care of my future. So please don't expect me to spend so much of money on such useless outings," Kuttan registered his displeasure on their way back.

Gowri laughed off his complaint and said, "Useless! Just one day of bill payment and these outings became useless for you. You are the one who earns between us and you still complain about money. You are such a miser looser," when it came to speaking out one's heart Gowri was as mean and as blunt as anyone could possibly be. She meant what she said and never regretted her words later.

Kuttan didn't speak anything. Gowri should have known that Kuttan needed money to pay his fees and build his life but, still she made fun of him. He felt hurt. Gowri could sense it. So, to make better sense of her point she said, "Let me tell you a story that my ammama used to tell."

'Once upon a time, long back there was a farmer who had a small pouch with best quality seeds of all the crops known to human and Gods. It was granted to him by Lord Brahma for his hard-work and dedication with utmost honesty.

The farmer wished to have the best possible result and earn lots of money out of them so as to secure his future. So he decided to wait till all the conditions became favourable. But always there was some hindrance to his perfect execution plan. Sometimes the rains were too less or sometimes there was a flood. Sometimes the soil lacked a few nutrients whereas sometimes there was pest problem. Sometimes the sun was too bright, sometimes the moon was too light. Sometimes the winds were not favourable then sometimes the time was not just right. So he waited for years. He suffered with his family using the limited resources while saving the best for the bright future later.

He waited and waited for many years. But, the ideal flawless conditions never came. Fed up of this waiting, his wife one day opened the pouch to sow them by herself. To her dismay all the seeds had rotten, covered with fungi they blackened.

The wait for the brightest future without investing in the present had blackened the farmer's present and future, alike, in to the darkness.

***

Gowri finished the story and asked Kuttan, "Understood something my dear looser friend."

"Hmmm…nice story. Quiet deep. I understood that you want me to spend money on you more frequently in the present. I understood that even your Gods give blessings with an expiry date. Also, one has to work really hard, be self-determined and make right decisions at the right time to become rich and successful. So, I will invest further more in to my dream," Kuttan said and walked ahead without waiting for Gowri's reaction.

"Really! Is this what you understood? Genius!" Gowri walked past him in to the class room with a disgusted look on her face. She went to her locker at the back took two hundred rupees out of her purse and offered it to Kuttan. It would have been so humiliating for any boy but, not for Kuttan; two hundred rupees were more important than his self-worth. He kept the money in to his shirt pocket.

"Thank you," he left without a hint of shame.

Chapter 15

The first Kiss

They didn't speak for a couple of days. Gowri thought of Kuttan's behaviour as selfish; she had a good reason to believe so. But, at heart she wanted to believe that she was wrong. It was his orphaned childhood with no one to take care that made him think about himself before anyone. She knew that Kuttan cared for her, he understood what she had been through. Although what she experienced was nothing when compared to what he had gone through but, she knew what it meant to have a 'lost' childhood. To be let down by parents who were supposed to carry them through tides of life without getting soaked in the gloom; they had failed them. Both were two souls having lost childhood, finding succour in the company of each other.

Kuttan was upset with her for what he believed was her arrogance of being rich and having parents to take care of her, *"What would she know how does it feel to be let down by loved ones? What does it mean to have a lonely childhood?"*

They still sat together, walked together, had lunch together but, didn't utter a word. The silence for both had different definition and meaning. They liked each-other's company. They cared for each other but were poles apart in the way and reasoning for their care. When Kuttan finally decided to break the silence his question was rather unexpected and came as a shock for Gowri, "Are you my girl-friend?"

"Sorry?"

"I mean, we are always together and we can't stay away even after a fight. So, does that mean there is more than just friendship between us?" Kuttan asked more cautiously reframing his question.

"Please don't spoil it. We like being together, have fun, find happiness even in the silly fight of ours but to interpret in any other way than friendship would ruin it. Being friends if we can have all the fun then why have any additional attachments? You know, the thing about our relation that I enjoy the most is freedom. The freedom to be what I am. I like you but please don't expect anything more from me," Gowri took the conversation quite seriously.

"Uff...Relax. These are not my doubts. I had just heard Surya ask this question to some students in our class. So, just asked you as I do usually," Kuttan didn't feel offended.

"Why would Surya enquire so?"

"No idea. Maybe you have been selected by the *Gandharvan* (the celestial lover) to be his next affection. You are the only girl who doesn't seem to be interested in him."

"Haha... not funny," she slapped him on his back with a smile and little shake of head.

Gowri was determined that this beautiful friendship would not be ruined like many other college friendships once they were solemnized by love. To have a beautiful girl care for him and befriend with her was more than what Kuttan had ever wished in his life. So, he didn't complain either but, not for long.

***

How long Kuttan could have waited before he wished and expected more from such a beautiful girl. In fact, for many Gowri was just an average girl. A girl with ordinary features. But for Kuttan she was a blessing; an extraordinary heart, which understood him and never tried to judge him. It was the latter quality that made her the most beautiful girl in his eyes.

One night after his job at the DTP centre as Kuttan waited for the bus, his Nokia phone rang. Gowri had gifted the phone to him. But Kuttan's busy schedule left him with little time to talk. This had become a sore point between them.

"I want to see you," Gowri demanded, "I mean now," she added after a pause.

"Hahaha... Are you crazy? I have to reach the ashram before night prayers," Kuttan dismissed the demand without asking the reason.

"I am not asking you, I am telling you. Tonight you would stay at my place. Treat this as a compulsion or I will come to your ashram at midnight."

"Either you are out of your mind or you are drunk," Kuttan didn't take her serious.

"I am not joking."

"Please do come at midnight. We organise rave parties at the ashram. I insist that you should join us. Oh! My bus has come," Kuttan disconnected the phone abruptly not before adding further sarcasm and ran for the bus.

***

At midnight the phone beneath Kuttan's pillow vibrated. He picked up the phone before anyone could realise the odd break in the pin drop silence. It was Gowri.

"What now, Gowri?" Kuttan whispered in a sleepy tone.

"How do I get in, the gate is locked?"

Kuttan's sleep was gone as if it had never happened in several years. His alertness would have put a military dog to shame.

"What? Are you crazy? Go back! You will get both of us killed. Please go," Kuttan cried and pleaded without any veil of self-esteem.

"Okay, I will jump the gate."

"Nooooo!!! Wait. I will come. Take the mud road on your left side to reach the back of ashram and wait for me and for my sake don't try to be over smart," Kuttan didn't hesitate to let her know of his disappointment.

Kuttan reached the back of ashram near the stable stealthily like a cat for her prey without even letting the voice of his fast beating heart disturb the silence. His breathe pattern were as calm as they always used to be but the sweat on his forehead failed him. He looked at Gowri with disbelief and anger. Gowri seemed oblivion to Kuttan's worries.

Kuttan showed her a small gap between the fences once created by an undisciplined calf which got stuck in there. The fence had to be cut on the sides to rescue it. The damage had not been repaired since then. A free spirited animal had made an opening for another one.

"How did you come?" Kuttan chose to neglect the warm smile, shake of hand and hi from Gowri.

"Auto," Gowri said bluntly without knowing the need for such a question.

"By auto. Are you nuts? Do you know how unsafe the autos are at night?"

"No."

"What do you mean by 'No'?"

"I mean this is for the first time I am out at night. So I don't know how dangerous it is. Also, I travelled in an auto because our places are not at walkable distance and I missed the last flight to your international ashram," Gowri was disappointed at the cold reception she had received at the hands of Kuttan.

"Why did you do this? Why are you here?" Kuttan tried to calm himself down.

"Shh…What's the time?" Gowri hushed him.

"It's five minutes less for the midnight."

"Oh god! Let's hurry. You help me," Gowri said with childish excitement.

"To do what? What is this all about? Please explain."

Kuttan stood there wondering what she was up to. Gowri went in to the stable took an old stool out. She kept a square box on to the table. Kuttan opened it as soon as he saw it. He could not stand the suspense anymore. He opened the box.

"Happy birthday MY Dileep"

Kuttan looked at her with disbelief in his eyes. He had never had a birthday cake in his life until then. He started crying. No one had ever put in so much of effort to make him feel special on this day or any day. The day laid back somewhere deep inside his memory almost untraceable. The day had ceased to exist once he begun to understand the relationship between his mother and Ramesh.

As a child his mother would take him to temple. She would ask him to pray and perform a *pushpanjali,* flower offering to the goddess, on the day. She would apply sandalwood paste on his forehead as Devi's blessing and then kiss him on his cheeks. The day was the only one in the year when something sweet would be prepared in his house. She would cook *payasam*, a dessert with rice and jaggery. But, that was somewhere long back in the past. Now the day didn't exist until Gowri reminded him.

What made him cry? Was it Gowri's care and compassion or were the memories of his mother and childhood days responsible? He was not sure. But he just could not control tears. The harder he tried to stop them the more they flowed out.

"Happy birthday! My special," this was closest to Gowri ever accepting that she loved him.

"Thank you," Kuttan was crying and smiling at the same time.

"Gowri! I think I love you," Kuttan could not resist but speak out the overwhelming emotions he was feeling for her.

"Shh... Don't spoil it. Now it's time for your birthday gift. Close your eyes."

Gowri moved close to Kuttan and kissed him softly on lips for a few seconds and then pulled back. Kuttan wanted more but didn't dare to ask, just kept his eyes closed for few more seconds feeling her soft lips over his. Gowri wanted it to last forever but unusually felt shy in his presence so turned her back to him. She had a steady deep breath and pleasure was evident in her half smile.

Kuttan moved close, held her tight by waist from behind and rested his chin over shoulder. He kissed her on the cheeks and said, "Thank you. I had lied to you when I said I think I love you. I know, I love you...very much...may be the most."

"Me too when I said don't spoil it. I loved it," Gowri tilted her head towards Kuttan, "I need to go back or it would be trouble if anyone finds out."

They slowly regained the senses after blissful silent confessions.

Kuttan walked her back to her home and took an auto back to the ashram to reach just in time for the morning duties. On their way they didn't speak a word, just the Good byes. Suddenly, words seemed to be incapable of expressing their feelings that were only possible for the eyes. Sometimes silence can convey what spoken words can't.

They, hand in hand, walked under the moon light stealing a glance in between at each other. The crickets were playing background score. The winds were whispering in the ears the magic of the moment. The long deserted roads were not frightening, they invited them to celebrate the moment of togetherness. They need not express their love in words because even a thousand words would have failed where these stealthy glances succeeded. They were in love and there was no denial of the fact. Just as always the meaning and interpretation were different respectively.

Chapter 16

Possessiveness for the possession

Kuttan believed that Gowri was his possession; her being in love with him justified his possessiveness. For Gowri, love was a source of liberation which provided immense happiness without any strings attached to it. Possessiveness, she believed, was like termite which feasted on the pulp of relations-trust. Once the trust was broken, the relationship too wouldn't survive.

Kuttan and Gowri were walking beneath the trees lining the college ground when a football flew past a tree and hit Gowri on her back. She fell down but didn't get hurt. Kuttan turned around furiously and saw an unapologetic guy standing a few feet away. He was Surya, a college stud who had huge fan following for his charming looks. Equally ill-famed were his relationships in college which hardly lasted few months at the most. He was one year senior to them but had failed to clear final year. Kuttan didn't like Surya, which was obvious in his frowned stare.

"Can't you be careful while playing?" Kuttan tried to be as furious as possible while helping Gowri on to her feet.

"Sorry Shaktiman! The balls are very disobedient," Surya came near them and kicked back the ball to the ground.

Kuttan heard a giggle, it was Gowri. She was least perturbed by the incidence. Surya winked at her and said, "Sorry dear. Hope you are alright."

"It's all right. I am fine. You carry on."

Kuttan was taken aback by her attitude towards him, "Don't repeat it."

"Ok Shaktiman!" Surya joked and left.

Kuttan again heard Gowri giggle. He impetuously held Gowri by her arm, "What's there to giggle so much?"

The hold hurt her- peripheral and deep.

"Need not explain it to you, and don't cross your limits," Gowri violently pushed aside Kuttan and stormed past him.

Kuttan's hate for Surya had increased exponentially.

Then the coincidences became more obvious and too frequent for Kuttan's comfort. Surya became part of 'their' friend circle. Kuttan had to agree as Gowri seemed to have no issues with it. They lunched together and went to Baskin and Robbins together unless Kuttan insisted otherwise.

One such evening Kuttan insisted Gowri that they should go out together, only two of them. They went to Marine Drive in Kochi. The sea shore lined with luxury apartments, pavements, trees, children's park and lined iron benches gave perfect view of the beauty of sea interspersed with islands which had five star hotels, with carved landscapes, on them. The walk-ways were crowded, the benches were mostly occupied, and the vendors were busy selling ice-creams, roasted ground nuts and attracting children with cheap china made toys, unsure of their longevity just like Kuttan and Gowri's relationship.

"Why do you have this new found interest in Surya?" Kuttan didn't care about people around, he was loud.

"Please keep your voice low. What interest are you talking about?" Gowri had widened eyes and hushed voice.

"I mean; what is he doing between us? Where ever we go he somehow manages to burrow in there," dislike for him were obvious in his words.

"Don't be silly. He only joins us for lunch and may be an occasional outing, that's it. He had told me that he wanted to be friends with us so that I can help him clear his final exams," Gowri tried to assure Kuttan that there was a reason for his new found interest.

"For that he can take tuitions. Don't befool yourself Gowri! He is interested in you and not your tuitions. I mean, you are no professor. And I think you too like him flirting with you."

"You are such a thankless creep! Don't forget you owe me your pass percentages for the past two years. Regarding flirting I could have easily had many guys flirt with me in the past two years? If it didn't happen then, it won't happen now either."

Kuttan kept quiet for some time. She spoke truth. She finished all the portions in two weeks advance and spoon fed them to Kuttan. She never gave any boy or girl more importance than him. She liked him for his innocence which slowly had begun to rust in the salty air of the city.

"He comes to the internet café, where I work, with 'many' girls. God knows what they do behind the closed doors," Kuttan tried to change the topic.

"Let them do whatever they want to, why should we bother? I am least interested to know," Gowri hated gossips.

"What do you mean? I think you didn't understand what I meant."

"I am not a toddler. I do understand what you mean, still I am not interested," Gowri looked irritated and her gesture with both hands jerking apart sidewise communicated to Kuttan that she was no longer interested in the topic.

Though Kuttan was still not convinced if she understood what happened behind those closed doors, he preferred to keep silent and let the sound of sea waves hitting against the rocks fill that silence; allowing the weeds of distrust and disrespect root between them.

***

Kuttan was roaming through the corridors of the college when his phone rang. It was his *maman* turned stepfather, Ramesh. The screen read *'xxxxxxx756 calling'*. Kuttan ignored the call after noticing last three numbers.

Chapter 17

Balikarmam

It had been sixteen days since the carrier of Uma's (Kuttan's mother) soul had been incinerated and relieved from this world of suffering. She was burned to ashes. The *asthi* were put in an earthen pot and placed at the south west end of the house. A lamp had been lit as a respect for the trapped soul in the pot.

The pot was usually kept at the place with lamp lit for one year before the *asthi* were dissolved in a water source. The cycle is thus completed. We are formed from five elements- *akasham, vayu, jalam, prithvi and agni*, and in the end converted in to the same.

On the sixteenth day, the son/ grandson will perform the ritual called, *balikarmam*; where rice balls and sesames seeds are offered to the crows. A Brahmin priest recites *mantras* for the salvation of the departed soul. The soul is believed to be trapped between the earth and heaven suffering by the guilt generated from the sins committed in this world. They continue to wander and suffer until the *balikarma* is performed by the son. The crow represents the soul waiting to be relieved and expresses the gratitude by accepting the offering. If the crow does not accept the offering then the soul is believed to be still attached to this world for some reason and do not wish for salvation.

Ramesh had explained the facts and beliefs behind the rituals to Kuttan. Kuttan did not know what to believe and what not to. If this was true then his father's soul should had been still around him, and, if it was so he would not have had such a miserable childhood. If this was false then his mother would be soon around him which he was not sure if he wished for? All the truths were relative to the Ultimate Truth one had faith in. What was Kuttan's faith? He didn't know. Either way he wished his parents to be together, if a world beyond existed, then he would someday be able to live with them, and be that four year old boy who had ceased to live but merely existed since then.

***

Kuttan's father, Mohammed Yusuf, was a noble man. He was a staunch believer in Allah and His goodness. The goodness which ought not to know any bounds of religion, caste or gender. The goodness which was rare to find. The goodness which attracted Uma, a Hindu Nair girl.

Uma's father a *jammi*, a traditionally wealthy landlord, didn't trust anyone with his beautiful daughter. He would get nervous with any man around her. In her father's rubber and cashew estate Yusuf worked as a driver. He trusted Yusuf more than any of his own. So he appointed Yusuf as her personal body guard cum driver. The choice was very cunningly sorted out.

Uma and Yusuf were poles apart. She was very beautiful whereas Yusuf was very ordinary. She was born and brought within the comforts of the bungalow of her father whereas Yusuf had seen all the colours and faced all the challenges the place could have offered. She was a secondary school failed and he could not even finish primary schooling. And above all, the mismatch was further reinforced by their respective faiths. So the match between two was impossible, almost.

For the two years when Yusuf was her driver, he was also her guide to the outside world. He took her out, showed the beautiful world and explained its mysteries. The birds which always chirped in her backyard but were never seen. The rivulets which she had heard but could never put her feet in. The mountains which seemed so far away from the comforts of her room. The waterfalls which she never knew could have existed. The beautiful nights which seemed so scary until then. He taught the meaning of life; the difference between living and existing.

For a girl born and brought up in the captivity and materialistic luxuries of the world. Yusuf was a discovery. It was just obvious for her to wish to spend the rest of her life with him. For Yusuf who had seen the beautiful world in its meanest possible form, Uma's angel like beauty, simplicity and innocence was something he had always dreamt of in his life partner. She believed in him blindly and he respected her immensely.

There was no question of asking the permission from the world which could not understand their love. He had an option to convert her to Islam and marry her. Thus, attaining eligibility for the protection from 'his' people. But, he had loved her for what she was and didn't wish to change her, even by a bit. So leaving their place for a faraway fair land where their identities would not have followed them was the only option. But such a land did not exist with humans around, they soon realised.

Uma was twenty at the time when they had eloped. She did not know many things about the world except what she had learned from Yusuf. She trusted Yusuf more than anyone, even her God. God gave her life but the meaning of life Yusuf had taught her. Until then, she had merely existed. She lived the life for the next five years with Yusuf. Then, she existed for the rest of her life under the shadows of those five years, waiting to be turned to ashes and the soul to be salvaged by her beloved son.

***

Kuttan stood in a wet towel after performing *bali* in the backyard of Ramesh's house, besides the *balichor* (offering of rice and sesames seed). He had no idea of what he was doing. He did as was told by the priest. Kuttan did not even know if he believed in these rituals. He performed all the rituals exactly as was told. He loved his mother a lot but could not spend a happy life with her.

"You have to clap the wet hands to invite the soul," Ramesh

said politely.

"You mean the crow," Kuttan shot back. The most painful part was Ramesh's presence. No matter how hard he had tried to forgive him, a child in Kuttan could never forgive Ramesh for stealing from him the right to his mother's love and care.

Clap...Clap...Clap...

A crow sat at a branch of the mango tree. It was looking at them. It must have had heard the claps but seemed hesitant to go near the *balichor.*

"The crow is there, it had been sitting there throughout the process. It might be afraid to come nearby. Let's move away from here," Ramesh suggested and moved along with the priest.

Kuttan stood there looking at the bird. He wanted to believe it was his mother's soul who was observing him. Then, why would she deprive him of his right to salvage her. He looked at the bird for as long as he stood there. It neither came near him nor flew away.

It started raining but Kuttan refused to move away. The balichor got washed away. The bird flew away to safety. Kuttan stood there staring at the banana leaf on the ground and remnants of rice and sesames seeds. The rain masked the tears that erupted from his eyes.

"You should have moved away from the *balichor,*" Ramesh said as he came near Kuttan with an umbrella.

"You should have never come in our lives," Kuttan pushed aside the help and left; wet outside yet burning dry and deep inside.

Chapter 18

The Tamarind Tree

The journey to Bengaluru by bus took more than twelve hours. It was first time that Kuttan had taken a luxury Volvo bus to Bengaluru. These changes were brought in Kuttan by Maya. It took her time, but it was huge as far as Kuttan was considered. He had begun to learn that money cannot provide security if not used for the intended purpose. She also taught him that there were more important things than money in this world.

As the bus was negating the serpentine curves of Western Ghats near Tamarassery on its way from Kozhikode to Wayanad, Kuttan was lost in his thoughts. How much did he love her? What goodness did he possess to have such a beautiful woman in his life? How she had transformed his life giving it a purpose. How she supported his ideas blindly; she had more trust in him than he himself had. The others were nauseating as bus negated the curves. Two persons were oblivion to the plight of others; one was Kuttan and the other was the driver.

Finally the bus stopped at a *dhaba*, a roadside restaurant on highways, underneath a huge tamarind tree. The *dhaba* was dimly lit with few bulbs and tube lights scattered around. There were some plastic tables and chairs set on the outside in the open and some were arranged inside a hall for families. The smell of tandoor and spices filled the air. There were not many people in the *dhaba* except for a few college boys who were probably on their way to Wayanad or may be Ooty or Bengaluru; the district shared border with both neighbouring states. The seats were arranged a bit away from the tree for the fear of birds on top of the tree ejecting there flavours in to the curry plates. From the corner seat where Kuttan sat, the tamarind tree seemed enormous as if a ghost had spread out its hands holding a blanket of darkness to engulf anyone who came in its vicinity.

As Kuttan had his *rotis*, Indian tandoor bread and *anda bhurji*, scrambled egg in excess oil and spices, he thought of a story once Gowri had told him about a tamarind tree in her village near Palakkad town. The tree was believed to be possessed by a *yakshi*, a female ghost, which engulfed any child who went near it and cried at night. She was a mother who had lost her child to a disease that came into the village during summer and preyed on the old, sick and young. All that anyone could remember were the cries of the poor woman breaking the silence of the dark night as the goddess embraced her child in to the dark hollow of her stretched arms. The devastated mother could not bear the pain and committed suicide by hanging herself to the tree which stood at the far end of the village. Since then any child who cried under the tree went missing. People believed the *yakshi*, consoled and secured them in to her protective lap.

Kuttan had wished to have such a possessed tree in his village which would have had engulfed him in to the love and security of a mother. But, not now. Now, he had an ambition and a loved one to share his dreams with. All of a sudden, he thought of his mother. A drop of tear rolled over his cheek in to the empty plate making a droplet over the oil in the plate. The horn of bus reminded him of his journey ahead. He had one last look at the tamarind tree. Now she was a motherly figure willing to embrace him. He smiled with moist eyes. He missed his mother.

***

Finally after three weeks, Kuttan reached back the society where he shared a flat with Maya on the eighth floor. This was a big one with more than two hundred families living there. Most were either retired high ranked government officials or belonged to NRIs which were rented out. It was a pleasant confluence of old and new, representing the spirit of the city.

Kuttan got the keys from the security who gave him a cold reception as he had done in the past. He stood up and saluted only those who came in expensive cars. He took the lift and pressed number eight. The slow lift reached the eighth floor. The veranda was empty. He opened the door and was surprised to see that the furniture of the room was sparse. He called the security and asked who told him that Maya had shifted the furniture to some other place which he had no idea of.

Kuttan called Maya but her phone was out of coverage area. She had told him that she would go and meet her mother to get the property papers so as to get the loan sanctioned. Kuttan knew that she had decided to move to a cheaper residential area to save money for their start-up project. She was getting ready for the struggle period. She too had changed. Kuttan was proud of her yet upset for deciding all by herself without consulting him; she never did. But for now, he was very tired to think about anything. He took bath and went to sleep.

"We have a few things to discuss when you reach back dear bossy girl," Kuttan muttered about to sleep knowing very well that he could not get mad with her whatever may be the reason. The eyelids became heavy, his eyes closed without any forewarning, and he slept with smile on his lips thinking of Maya.

Chapter 19

The Most Attractive Woman

When Kuttan woke up after the nap it was already dark. The sun had gone hiding as the darkness loomed over him in the room. The yellow street lights faintly coloured the room. The white netted curtains were blowing slowly in the evening breeze. The silence in the room seemed as if it was there to stay for long. His head seemed heavy and eyelids heavier. He took a few deep breathes and exhaled forcefully to push out the feeling of doom that tried to creep in to him. Kuttan felt lonely, he missed Maya.

Kuttan decided to go to Club 7 pub where he had met Maya for the first time. Kuttan hired a taxi to the 100 feet road where the pub was situated. It is one of the newer happening areas of the city; the kind of places which Kuttan avoided unless she insisted. He felt very uncomfortable in the presence of noisy happy people. His discomfort however had decreased over the past year when Maya had brought him there frequently for dinner; hard-core parties they both avoided.

For the first time Kuttan visited the place alone. The pub was lit with red, purple and white lights just enough to guide him to his favourite couch at the right far corner. A group of college students were having fun at the other corner. Kuttan smiled at them, strangely he felt nice and not jealous.

***

It was during a birthday party Kuttan had first met Maya. The whole pub was booked for the private party. It was Surya's birthday, the guy behind his and Gowri's breakup. Two years, later he was celebrating his foe's birthday at the insistence of his ex-girlfriend. What a sorry state he was in! It was then that she had noticed him on the couch. He still could not believe his good luck that Maya noticed him in the party which had about fifty 'beautiful' people. The least attractive guy had attracted the most attractive woman in the party.

As Maya reached near the table, Kuttan found himself incapable of looking at her. He was sitting there for the past one hour wondering about his presence there. But, now he was aware of the surroundings. He could hear the music beats, the laughs and the noise; he was sitting right there in the middle of all the fluctuations. He realised that he had been sipping a glass of drink for one hour. He was aware that a beautiful attractive woman was standing beside his table, her legs were thin and long. He kept staring at them out of fear to meet her eyes or may be even out of mere admiration, even he was not sure. The way she stood there, he knew she was confident about herself; exactly the kind of people Kuttan had tried to avoid his whole life.

"I think you have stared enough to look up now," Kuttan heard a mesmerising confident voice.

Kuttan looked up and now he could not take his eyes of her face; his breath had slowed down a bit with heart trying to pump out of his chest. Her big black lined eyes constantly followed his gaze. Her left half face would get covered by few strands of hair which she regularly pushed aside, all while maintaining the eye contact. Her mischievous smile revealed that she enjoyed making Kuttan uncomfortable. She said something but all Kuttan could see were her perfectly aligned teeth stretching out just enough beneath the slightly everted lips under the sharp nose. She wore a purple knee length skirt with a magenta coloured sleeveless top. The dress revealed that she had a perfectly chiselled body.

"Hi I am Maya," she leaned close to Kuttan to be audible and sat near him. The heart, which was trying to break out from the chest wall the last minute had now almost refused to beat.

"I think I should leave. Maybe you prefer to be alone," after waiting for few moments Maya was about to leave when Kuttan cleared his throat and said, "No. Please stay back. I am sorry, I was just lost in thoughts. I am Dileep," all said in one breathe.

"Woof... you speak with some speed. Don't you? I am sorry, but I didn't get your name, it's so loud here."

"Dileep."

"Hi again Dileep. Why don't you join your friends on the floor?"

"Not interested. Actually, I feel kind of a misfit among them," Kuttan said wrinkling his forehead and biting the lower lip, "Why are you wasting your time here around me?"

"Let me decide that. If we both are not interested here, let's move out. Do you mind walking down few streets?" She suggested knowing very well Kuttan would oblige.

"Why not? Let's go. I have nothing left in this party anymore," his eyes stopped on Gowri, busy dancing with new group of friends, for a moment then turned to the beauty beside him. They walked out pass a few envied eyes. Kuttan enjoyed all the attention he derived as they walked out of the pub. Probably for the first time in his life someone had envied him.

They walked through the busy streets in to a residential area. It was not too late yet only a few people were present on the road as a slight drizzle was there which either of them failed to notice. Kuttan said nothing still wondering what this beauty was doing with her antonym.

"What are you thinking?" Maya asked reading his mind.

"Nothing. Just..." Kuttan still could not open up.

"I don't like loud parties. Only you in the party seemed least interested in there, so I came to you. Just wanted to get out of there."

"Why did you come to the party then?" Kuttan asked without looking at her.

"A friend insisted," she replied casually, "and you?"

"Ex-friend insisted," Kuttan still looked down.

"Ex- girlfriend?" Maya smiled looking at him.

"Don't know," the smile could not hide the disappointment within.

"Don't worry. Just asked, not interested. I have had my share of past," she still looked at Kuttan, "Am I boring you? I think I am, or else you would have looked at me at least once in the past half an hour," Maya had ran out of patience.

"Please let me decide that. Actually I have never been with anyone as beautiful as you before. So I don't know what to say or do, how to behave?" Kuttan looked at her for a brief time then looked down hurriedly.

"Wow. That's so cute. Thank you Dileep. This is the most honest compliment anyone has ever said to me," Maya was happy and it was evident in her smile as she looked down.

"What do you do?" Kuttan changed the subject as he had no idea about how to proceed from there.

"I am an IT graduate pursuing MBA at the Presidency," Maya talked without any interest in the topic.

"I am…" Kuttan was about to speak when she interrupted, "To be honest I am least interested in discussing academics or career."

They had walked past the remaining residential area in silence to once again reach a busy road. They exchanged phone numbers then hired taxies. He went to the university college hostel and she went to her flat. Kuttan wondered throughout the ride if it was real or some kind of dream. Although Kuttan pinched himself to blissfully realise that it was a truth, but his mind still cautioned his heart of going down the smitten lane.

Chapter 20

The Project Messaging

Kuttan waited for two days for a message from her, then he ran out of patience. He could not stop thinking about her lined black eyes, her red everted lips lining a mysterious smile, her tanned skin tone, her purple-magenta dress, the smell of her perfume. The mind kept on warning but the heart just could not stop thinking of her. The harder he tried, more he thought of her. The more he thought of her, more attractive she became. The more attractive she became, the more he liked her. He didn't complain.

With great courage, Kuttan decided to message her instead of calling. He was afraid of the possibility that Maya might fail to remember him.

"Hi Maya.

This is Dileep. We met at Club 7 two days back.

Hope you remember.

How r u?"

Kuttan sent the message not before deleting it for three times. Typing three lines took thirty minutes, sending another thirty. Then the wait began. It continued for another week. Kuttan would check his inbox every hour only to be disappointed.

All of a sudden the city seemed beautiful. The city that was too large and noisy couple of days ago seemed a nice place to be in now. The polluted air and dust had settled down. Kuttan found that there were lot of greenery and gardens in the city. The multitude of roads and confusing fly overs had simplified access to Hi-Life apartments in Bellandur. He realised that water scarcity and waste disposal were a common menace to any city in the country. The people became polite and the Kannada language didn't seem too difficult to learn. He had committed to learn a language without even knowing if she was a Kannadiga. The idea of finishing PG course and moving back to Kerala seemed unnecessary. Everything seemed so perfectly beautiful except for the fact that she had not replied.

Two weeks after they had met, Maya messaged Kuttan.

"Hey Hi!!!

Dileep.

I remember. I am good.

How are you?

I was not in Bengaluru, had gone to Pune.

Glad you messaged."

Kuttan had read the message the moment it was delivered and then reread a couple of more times. But he decided to not to reply immediately or it would seem he was desperate. He would have replied only after one day if he was to listen to his mind but since the heart had begun to rule him, his resistance lasted only half an hour. He replied back.

"Pune? So are you Marathi?"

"Work?"

She replied immediately.

"Nope. My family is there."

"Ohh... K," Kuttan didn't want a discussion on family so he didn't ask anything further.

"I use a separate number in Pune. My family doesn't know about this number."

"Y so?"

"You ask too many questions."

"Ohh... I am sorry. Just asked."

"Shall tell you next time when we meet."

"Won't bother u wid stupid questions nxt time v meet. Promise."

"HaHa…You better not. Have to go for now, catch you later."

"When shall v meet?

Ohh… Busy? Sorry no questions!

Hmm…Bye. Tc. C u."

The fact that Maya had replied boosted Kuttan's confidence. She had suggested that they should meet again. Although the conversation seemed formal, but Kuttan wished to believe that she too was eager to meet him. The best part of listening to one's heart is that it speaks exactly the words which you wish to listen unlike mind which sends useless unnecessary warnings.

Meanwhile, he sent her a friend request on Facebook.

Kuttan visited library during every break to check his FB account. His 'friends' in college, Gowri and Surya, had enquired several times.

"Just working on a project," Kuttan replied.

"What project are you working on? We also study the same course; how come we don't have any project?" Surya got suspicious, "Is it related to some girl?" he teased him.

"Why don't you mind your own job? If I have anything to discuss, I will let you know; both of you," Kuttan made sure he registered his displeasure with the exact person he intended to.

"Ok. Let's go Surya. If you have anything worth discussing don't hesitate. We were friends and shall always remain so," Gowri still cared for Kuttan but decided to let him have his space rather than imposing her friendship on him.

"You leave your friends for a new girl?" Surya was sure about sudden change.

"There is no girl; and please don't teach me moral. You don't have any rights," they disliked each other more than even either of them knew.

"Do you want to know my rights?" Surya held Kuttan by his collar.

"Please stop. Both of you. Not again. I have tolerated enough of this drama between you both," Gowri interfered.

"Who has asked you to tolerate? Leave me alone. I don't need anyone, especially you!" Kuttan meant what he said.

"You will suffer for this boy," Surya said to console his ego like many times before but Gowri won't let him harm Kuttan.

"Leave him Surya. You would never hear anything from us again," Gowri's eyes spoke that she was hurt.

"I don't want to. I can survive without you," Kuttan looked straight in to her eyes. He had yearned to say this for long.

***

When checked in the evening, Kuttan's inbox had messages. It was Maya, she was online.

"Hi Dileep!

My friends are again planning for a party this weekend. I am not interested.

Do you know anyone who is not interested in partying and may join me for a movie?"

"Haha… I know a poor guy who can come, if u wish."

"I love charity. Ask him to come. My treat."

"Place? Which movie?"

"PVR Koramangala… Friday… 8:00 pm."

"Ok Mam!"

"Haha… Good boy. See you then."

"Can't wait."

"Just two days. Bye."

"Bye. Tc."

Chapter 21

The First Date

Kuttan reached the Forum mall at 7:30 pm and as usual waited for her. He wandered through the mall. For a moment a thought of buying Maya a gift passed through but since the financial matters still needed mind's consent, he dropped the idea. There were so many attractions in the mall that even roaming without a purpose would have cost five hundred rupees to any other person but Kuttan; he had earned every single paisa in his life by struggle, hard work and financial discipline or as Gowri used to say, being hopelessly miser. He just roamed around for some time till he got bored and then waited in front of the multiplex hoping for a wonderful romantic outing, better than the last one.

The movie was to play on screen 1 at 8:30 pm. It was a Hindi movie, *Margaret with a straw*. Maya had booked tickets. She stayed at a place of less than an hour travel. Hiring a taxi was the most convenient mode of transport in the city which ensured safety and punctuality but still Kuttan was eager. When he called she didn't respond. Then he left a message- *"waiting in the lounge of theatre."*

The movie didn't have any superstars; Kuttan realised as he looked at the posters. It was beyond Kuttan's intelligence how could a movie succeed without a male lead. These thoughts were passing through his mind when he heard the mesmerising voice again, "Hope you didn't get bored."

Kuttan turned around to find Maya dressed in a white jeans and pink T-shirt. He discovered a black mole on her chin just below the lower lip on left side that he had failed to notice the other night. His eyes were stuck on her when she indicated in action that it was already late. She pulled him by arm and moved towards the screen 1. His eyes moved from her face on to the arms holding his. Kuttan loved the authority she showed over him.

During interval the boys wearing caps came to the seat to take orders. Maya ordered two popcorns, Swiss rolls and cool drinks which cost her over five hundred rupees. Kuttan was amazed how extravagantly she spent money. He felt a bit odd, a kind of feeling he never had with Gowri.

Throughout the movie Maya kept her hand close to Kuttan's on the arm rest of the seat. Gowri had once told him that a girl would only hint at what she wanted and a smart man should read those signs. Was this an indication to hold her hand? Did she feel emotionally vulnerable during the movie? When he looked at her she was looking at the screen without a blink. Kuttan slowly moved his hand close to her just enough to touch on the side, it was so wonderfully warm. She still didn't move her eyes of the screen. With lot of effort Kuttan took her arms in to his, his heart was beating at inhuman pace. She looked at Kuttan, her eyes blinked. She didn't respond. She moved close, they watched the remaining movie unmoved.

They didn't speak for some time after the movie as they walked to a nearby restaurant for dinner. Maya ordered food for both of them. They still didn't discuss anything about the movie.

"So, did you like the movie?" Kuttan started the conversation. Time spent with Gowri had helped Kuttan to understand and open to women better.

"Nope. I mean it's a good movie, but I didn't like it."

"Hmm... Did I do something that spoiled your mood?"

"No Dileep. You have been very sweet. Just didn't like the way they oversimplified things. Do you think life is so easy for a girl in our society? How many mothers do you know who support their children so passionately to follow their passion, leave a disabled girl but a normal one?"

"I don't know, maybe I agree. I wish I had such a mother. By the way, life is not easy for boys too, they too struggle a lot," Kuttan replied in a low voice, last part audible only to self.

"Such understanding parents exist only in movies and stories. You know something, I want to do fashion designing but I am stuck in this stupid IT thing. My mother and brother are running a relatively successful business in Pune. They want to expand the business so I need to join them after I finish my MBA. I just don't like a thing about corporate but still I have no choice."

"I don't know what to say? I never had anyone to advice or force me to do anything."

"I know. Lucky you. You are self-made. I admire you so much for that."

"I won't wish my luck for anyone. I am nothing but a struggler, possibly a loser."

"I vehemently disagree. I really wish we could switch our lives."

"Me too."

They had most of the dinner in silence. Even though Kuttan insisted, Maya paid the bill. It had become a thing worth notice between them, whenever they talked to each other they felt emotionally vulnerable yet liked each other's company; they would enjoy the warmth of mutual respect and concern over the silence between them.

As she hired a taxi to leave, Kuttan asked, "Was it a date?"

Maya came close to him, smiled and kissed him on his cheek. "Don't know, maybe. Why did you ask?"

"Just... I am afraid of getting used to any goodness around me, it doesn't last for long."

"Then better get used to, life is never the same always. Bye," Maya pinched his cheeks and left; leaving behind the universal Maya of women. Kuttan stood their thrilled waving at the passer by, still confused trying to comprehend the incomprehensible.

***

Chapter 22

Time and Woman

Sixty seconds in a minute, sixty minutes in an hour, twenty four hours in a day, three hundred sixty five days in a year and a few such years in a life- time should be the most rigid thing in the universe. The truth is that the time is the most flexible and unfathomable thing in the universe, guided by the relativity theory. Not relative to the space and gravity as the scientists would like us to believe but relative to the feelings in our heart and how do we treat them, possibly only a woman's heart is comparable to it.

Time is a slave for a day, it turns in to a master the other. A woman is someone's biggest weakness and she can be his greatest strength as well. Time guides you in to the future one day, it misguides you to the past guilt the other. A woman can help him scale all heights of success and she can throw him in to the craters of failure as well. Time flows like stream one day, it is motionless like a stagnant gutter on the other. A woman is a volatile scent spreading sweet smell when set free; she would disintegrate in to fumes of pungent displeasure when caged against her will. Time is the joy of love one day, it is the pain of separation on the other. A woman is the love of mother and sweetheart; she is also the repugnance and envy of a hater. Time is hope for a day, it is despair on the other. A woman is the hope of peace and compassion for future when she was the cause of the wars in the past.

The women in Kuttan's life were as unfathomable as time was. Mother who had loved him the most, left him unattended to struggle through the childhood, and chose a life for herself. The women Balan had affair with, seemed to have everything possible for a comfortable life but naively believed in flattery of a guy with the lowest of morals possible. Gowri, the rebel girl, with the most loving heart neither admitted her love nor stopped caring. Just when Kuttan thought he could control her she slipped away from his life like the sand between the fingers on the *Cherai* beach where they went to see a sea, for the first time in his life.

Now, there was Maya; one of the most attractive person to have come across Kuttan's life. A woman who could make the best men nervous approached a man who would become nervous in the company of any woman. A woman whom most men would have desired in their fantasies admired and kissed a man who was a loser in his own eyes.

The more Kuttan tried to understand the puzzle of time and women in his life the more baffled he became. He was loving every moment of time spent with the woman, Maya. He decided to enjoy the passion of love, Maya and the time spent with her filled in the air around him. There was nothing much to understand but to just breathe in the air and enjoy the freshness it brought.

***

Six months in to their relation, Maya wished to share with Kuttan her favourite place on earth. It was a secret in her life none of her friends or family knew about until then; only Mats knew about it, which was his original secret.

Maya's family had a coffee, palm and areca nut plantation near a small temple town of *Kollur* in the valleys of unexplored Western Ghats. The plantation extended many acres. It belonged to a British company which later went on to its Indian caretaker. The children of the owner studied in convent went to UK for higher studies and had settled there. They wished to dispose of the plantation which was constantly neglected and generated financial losses. It shared its boundaries with the Tiger Reserve which made the place a poor deal. When Maya heard about the place last year from one of her friends, a real estate agent, she pressed her mother to buy it. Thus Maya became the owner of the property, no one else was interested in it.

The plantation was about eight hours drive from Bengaluru city. Maya decided to drive up to the place in her red SUV. She used to go there alone whenever she felt sad and lonely; this time she had other reasons.

Few kilometres before reaching Kollur, an off road drive of three kilometres uphill through the fog along a fenced boundary which was parallel to the dense forest with humungous trees and deep penetrating sounds of a flowing stream, chirping birds in the evening, crying crickets and many more unrecognisable. The fence ended in front of a large wrought iron gate which opened on to a stoned path leading to an old, recently renovated wooden cottage.

The gate was closed. At the sound of horn an old man in his eighties reached the gate. He moved too swiftly for his age. His name was Mathew Thomas. Maya used to call him Mats. He was not surprised to see Kuttan with Maya. She had told Mats about him last time when she visited alone.

"Welcome Madam and Dileep Sir," Mats said without any apprehension.

"You know my name?" Dileep was puzzled.

"I am an old man who knows many more things sir," Mats mumbled as he moved slowly in to the cottage with the luggage, the speed somehow was replaced by a tired gait.

"After you my esteemed guest," Maya teased Kuttan with half bent forward gesture.

Kuttan smiled shyly and did as was expected of him.

Chapter 23

Secretive Adventure
with a Loving Friend…

Next day morning after break-fast Kuttan overheard Maya and Mats discussing about him in the Kitchen.

"Are you sure he can be trusted? Is this important?" Mats sounded doubtful.

"Yes. I am sure. You can trust him like me," Maya reassured Mats.

"I have kept this place a secret for the past seventy years. I was just ten when I discovered this place. I used to go there when my *Mamaji*, maternal uncle, used to starve me. I used to catch fishes and cook them in my den. You can do as you wish. I told you about the place because I felt being important to someone, and found some-one willing to listen to me without considering me crazy for the first time in my life. I have had quite a long life. Haven't I?" Mats had tears in his eyes while remembering those painful days when his mother had left him with his newly rich *Mamaji*. He was ten. India had got independence 'at the stroke of midnight' which Mats came to know of very late; not that it mattered to him anyhow. He still starved, he was still beaten blue, he still had to do all the household works, and he still was an unwanted soul until Maya brought the property and found him. They developed a strong bond after they spent the first night there together. She loved to hear his stories and he enjoyed telling his tales of existence. One such fairy tale like place existed and was known only to Mats which he had told Maya, not just out of affection but also by the desire of leaving behind his legacy. The idea that Maya was about to reveal it to anyone else unsettled him.

"Don't worry, your secret will be with safe with me. I promise, I won't tell him how to trace the place? But I too am fed up of my lonely life. I think I have found someone worth loving and living for. I look up to him and wish to be there with him. Hope you understand," Maya palpated the scar of log burn on his forearm to calm him.

Mats kept looking through the kitchen window beyond the garden in to the valley. He didn't say anything.

Maya left.

***

Maya and Kuttan, with their backpacks, walked past the coffee plantation up till the farthest end. The plantation ended with picket fencing. Many similar looking wooden logs were arranged vertically and horizontally. Every piece of the fencing looked ridiculously symmetric; in actual it was set smartly symmetric on purpose by Mats. Maya moved straight towards a log and walked past removing and later replacing it. The boundary between forest and plantation was diffused, extremely difficult to make out the difference. But Maya treaded quite easily; Mats had trained her well.

Kuttan followed.

"Do you know what the foremost secret of access to the place is?"

"No. How would I know?"

"It is accessible only from this side."

"You mean from the plantation."

"To be more specific, from point we made entry. From any other point you will get lost."

"But how did you make out which one was the correct log?"

"Sorry, I am not supposed to tell you."

Maya slipped down the slope efficiently tackling the bushes

and branches. Kuttan followed her less efficiently hence getting bruised and pricked in the process.

"Don't worry this will hurt only initially."

"Then?"

"Then you will get used to it," Maya laughed aloud at her own joke.

"Haha...hilarious but too old a joke," he mocked her.

Kuttan was thrilled and excited.

Maya was looking up in between as if looking for some sign on the tall trees. Then she stopped abruptly and turned left. Kuttan had absolutely no idea how she was tracing the place but he was enjoying the apprehension and enthusiasm of discovering something new. A feeling he had rarely experienced, pleasant one. Everything seemed so wonderful.

"Are you sure, there is no other way? I mean Mats could have lied to you."

"Why would he lie? If he had to lie then why would he reveal it to me? You should trust people a bit more. Moreover, nobody knows this jungle better than him."

"Well, I think you are being unfair to me. I am following someone in to the deep jungle without knowing the destination. If that's not trust, what else is?"

Maya looked back above her shoulder and smiled. She loved the trust he had shown in her, "So then, shut up and follow me. We are only half way down."

"Hmmm...Yes madam."

They reached at the end of a vertical slope down to which laid a dense green black carpet covered valley on three sides by many feet vertically high hills. The only separation at the apex of the tri-angle formation was a white lined noisy water fall.

"Is that waterfall, the place?"

"There lies the second secret. Anyone even if somehow reaches this place would be mesmerised and misguided by the noise of the waterfall and will fail to trace the silent beauty lying above it. Only a soul desperately looking for solace in solitude could have found this place, hence Mats did."

"We have reached so far deep in to the jungle! I admit that I am a bit frightened."

"Don't worry. These jungles have only tigers as big cats which are very rare. But the most dangerous animals out here are bison. They can be very unpredictable."

"That's worst comforting I have ever heard! What if any of those things come across?"

"Nothing. Just change your direction silently without giving any undue importance to its presence. That's what Mats had told me."

"Great! That's so simple for me. First time I am thankful for my dark colour," Kuttan tried to hide his anxiety behind the self-pity.

Maya and Kuttan climbed past the waterfall using a rope that was hidden underneath the shallow stream by Mats. Few more meters uphill they reached a spring with bluish green water shining in the noon sun. The sunrays through a window in the sky amidst tall trees reached the pond, sparkling the water. There were lots of monkeys around, seemed a little disturbed by the invasion of their space by intelligent cousins. Butterflies of all known colours to Kuttan were flying in random around and sat on the rock walls. A small stream poured constant amount of water which seemed to be seeping through the rocks.

A small hole on the rock wall about ten feet to the left side of the stream was completely hidden behind wild berry bushes. Maya slid through the hole inside in to a slit and asked Kuttan to do the same. Kuttan followed hesitantly. The slit was hardly wide enough to hold both of them inside. Their sweaty bodies rubbed against each other. Her breasts on his chest, waist over waist, thighs over thighs, breathe over breathe, anxiety over nervousness, passion over passion, madness over madness. He could smell her strawberry lipstick. Out of nowhere the magic in the atmosphere conspired for a moment, Kuttan kissed her.

"There is a much better place beyond this, let's go," Maya too wanted him to hold her but not so inconveniently, she slid past him.

As they moved a meter into the slit it widened in to a spherical area as if the rock was hollow from inside. Similar slits but only few inches wide surrounded the rock cavity. They illuminated the crater as if millions of fireflies conjoined together at the centre scattering their light spreading across the horizon. The crater beneath seemed the extension of green water spring in to the heart of the rock or was this the source of the spring and stream outside, it was hard to make out. The water was more dark green which sparkled intermittently.

"Can you swim?" Maya threw her back pack in to the water and asked.

"Yes...but..."

Splash...

Maya jumped in to the water. Kuttan stood there amazed, trying to imbibe the beautiful moment.

Chapter 24

Secretive Adventure
with a Loving Friend, continued…

Maya swam calmly with the backpack to the sloped rock shore. Kuttan still could not believe his eyes that such a place could exist. He stood awestruck. Maya had always been an amazement to Kuttan which increased many folds during this trip. Her driving, her compassion for a lonely old man, the beauty of mysterious nature, the smell and the softness of her lips, the beauty of her dripping wet body; Kuttan was possessed.

Kuttan stood there looking at her without blinking. Maya went behind an extension of rock that stood as a partial partition, she changed in to her blue swim suit and slowly merged in to the beauty of the spring. She swam as elegantly, for his eyes, only a mermaid could have in some fairy tale.

"Is this deep?" Kuttan wanted her attention.

"Very deep and very cold," her eyes invited Kuttan to jump in to the spring.

Kuttan threw his backpack in to the water and jumped. He felt as if an ice-cold lightening went through him. He swam hurriedly through the spring to the shore gasping for air. He shivered at the shore as Maya laughed enjoying the poor plight of Kuttan; she loved his innocence, she loved directing him with her beautiful aura.

"How can you swim in this cold so calmly?"

"Don't worry its cold only for the first time then it becomes much warm. If you wish you can light a fire, there are firewood behind that stone wall," Maya seemed to be enjoying the cold water much to the amazement of Kuttan.

Kuttan lit the fire and tried to warm himself. He didn't dare to go in to the water again so he sat watching the beauties of nature enjoying each other. Maya didn't force Kuttan to join, she enjoyed teasing Kuttan. After much self-persuasion Kuttan went in to the water. To his wonder Maya was right, the water felt warm and she felt warmer. They swam together playfully until they could not anymore, then dried themselves changed to the dry clothes and sat beside each other near the fire, arms crossed and her head over his shoulder.

"Why did you bring me here when Mats was against the idea?"

"Two things. First, over hearing is bad manners. Second, the answer you must have already heard, sorry... overheard."

"Is this real or some kind of joke? I mean look at you! What are you doing with me?"

"You are such a mood spoiler. I know what you mean. You are afraid that I might dump you," Maya moved a little away.

"Please don't get me wrong. The experiences I have had in my life been such. Whom-so-ever I had loved the most, had been possessive about, they were the people who had hurt me the most."

Maya moved close to Kuttan and kissed him softly, "Then don't try to possess them, love them. You know what attracted me about you? Your innocence in this cunning crowd. I had been around such fake caring, loud and too expressive people for long only to realise it all lasted only as long as you were important and needed by them. You are different, you are independent. You are here by your own efforts. I admire it so much. I felt you were silently but constantly moving towards realising your dreams. After I met you I dared to dream again. A dream I had almost given up. Now, I too wish to be free in my life, without anyone to make decisions for me for their sake. Without a mother to love me to feel less guilty of pushing for divorce and possessing me without even sharing with dad. Without a brother who never had any ambitions or hopes in life hence didn't let me chase mine. I wish to be with you, see you, and listen to you. I feel free with you. That's it!" she tried hard to hide her disappointment but the eyes outpoured her pain. She felt relieved.

Kuttan moved close, held tight and said, "I love you," he kissed her, first softly then passionately.

"Me too," she kissed him back, feeling light and free in his arms. He kissed her over her neck, shoulders and ears while his hands moved up and down her body, exploring the beautiful curves he had been so passionately observing. But, when he tried to undress her, she resisted; she was not ready. He respected her feelings more than his desire for love making. He obliged.

As the dusk approached, it begun to get dark in there. The light from fire illuminated the place as lavishly as possible for a homeless on the street and as miserly as possible for a super-rich in his palace.

"When shall we leave, it's getting dark?" Kuttan asked hesitantly.

"In the morning, after it's bright. It's not safe to walk the jungle in the dark," Mats had told her.

"So we sleep hungry tonight?"

"Not necessarily. I have some snacks in my bag. If you want more, there are crabs in some of those small slits and fishes trapped in smaller satellite ponds."

"Hmmm... I think snacks will do," Kuttan replied shyly understanding the taunt.

They both spoke and laughed whole heartedly as if trying to flush out a life time of miseries from within. Then they slept in their sleeping bags looking at each other until their eye lids could no longer hold them between them; they beheld each other in to dreams.

On their way out, next morning in the slit, Kuttan held her tight again and said, "Sorry for the question last night and thank you for trusting me so much."

"You should try to trust people. You are a much better human being than you think you are, and hence you will surely find what you have been seeking for," she leaned up towards him and kissed softly, "Thank you for keeping my trust and not spoiling the most beautiful night of my life."

Kuttan didn't understand exactly what she meant but felt proud that he could make her happy. He followed with eyes stuck on her. They trekked their way back up to the plantation carrying over the mesmerising silence of the rock cave with them.

Chapter 25

Destination, a Maya

Maya had a heart which loved without bounds, without heeding to rules of love set around in the hypocrite world. Every time she loved wholeheartedly anyone, they had let her down.

She loved her dad as a child more than anyone but his priorities were journalism and activism, so much so that her mother willingly lost him forever to the activism hunger over the business wealth of her parents. They got divorced when she was six. She had, since then, seen her dad scarcely before he was shot dead by some gangster in broad daylight in Mumbai. She was ten. She still remembered his smiling face and how much she adored and admired him as his little princess.

They had moved to Pune with her maternal grandparents to run their computer hardware business. Her mother and brother were sucked in to the business vacuum by their desperation to rectify her mother's mistake of loving a non-worthy man blindly. Maya disagreed about her father being non-worthy, but it didn't matter. Although Maya never complained but she believed it was her mother's mistake; she loved him but still didn't trust their relation. Her mother tried a lot to compensate for the lack of love with lots of luxury, little she knew how much the father was missed by her child.

Maya loved her brother for sacrificing his adolescence. She always looked up to him for support. He failed to support her dream to become a fashion designer. He saw her as a key to expand their newly started software business.

The school friends failed to understand her love for two guys in the same school. One she was proud to be seen around with for his good looks and other she admired for his wittiness and caring nature. She just could not understand why she should choose between two; she had two boyfriends. After lots of harassment by peer and a label of 'whore', she understood that love and relationship came as a package. One just can't selectively choose the good from a person and ignore the bad. She had to accept the person as a whole, which had been cumbersome for her.

Kuttan was thus a chosen package for inspiration, self-determination, care and trust, even though he lacked the conventional qualities of a heart-throb. It was first time that she genuinely tried to be satisfied with what she had in her life.

"Would you like to share my apartment? My flatmate got transferred," Maya asked Kuttan as they had ice cream after a movie in the mall. He had finished his masters' course in computer science, and joined an IT multinational company.

"Hmm... I would love to, but it is beyond me. It's too costly," Kuttan replied after a brief pause.

"Do I look like in need for money? You are such a stupid. I need your company. I want to spend more time with you."

"I know. But I can't stay without paying my share." Kuttan had begun to change.

"You can pay it later when you get a better job."

"I wish I could but you know that's not practical."

"Ok we can do one thing. Our cook has left too. I know you are a good cook, so in that way you have to pay only five thousand after deducting the salary of the cook. What do you say?" Maya genuinely wanted to spend as much time with him as was possible.

"Hmmm...I think that may work out," Kuttan sported a broad smile. He too wanted to be with her but not at the cost of his self-respect which Maya had took care off just then. Moreover, he had lived all his life thus far to save money, now he wished to live for love.

"Great! That's like my good boy. I love you so much," Maya loudly announced. She got super-excited, felt triumphant and kissed him on his cheeks. Kuttan looked around embarrassed wiping off the chocolate of his cheeks, silently trying to convince the least bothered people around that he was not responsible for such a reaction.

***

Kuttan shifted to the Hi-Life apartments next week. It was the first time that he had come to her place. He was dumbstruck as he entered the society. Four two hundred feet tall towers loomed over him casting shadows over his sweaty head. Maya waved and smiled from the balcony to him, which calmed his nerves and satisfied the piercing looks and questions of the security guard.

The security had his reasons for suspicion. Kuttan carried an old suitcase and backpack along with the old trunk which none of the civilised upper class would use, definitely not in such a posh society. Kuttan's inferiority complex was reinforced by the suspicious security guard.

As he entered the building and walked towards the lift he was amazed by the extravagance. The floors had expensive pure white marbles ending in a central open area with a copper brown sculpture within its boundaries- a mother breast feeding her child. Next to the area was the lift; he took the lift. Maya waited outside the flat and cheerfully welcomed her partner.

"Hey! Wow… Cool trunk."

"Your security doesn't agree with you, I guess," Kuttan smiled carrying the luggage along.

"Leave him, he is an idiot. Did you find it difficult to find the place?" That was just a formal question, all the taxi drivers in Bengaluru knew the place.

"No it was not difficult," equally formal was the reply.

"Oh I am sorry. Come in. Welcome home my partner… cum cook," Maya winked and rubbed on his back.

"Ha-ha..." Kuttan laughed.

It was a 3 BHK apartment. Two rooms had balconies. One Maya had occupied and the other was waiting for Kuttan. The whole apartment was well furnished except the room which Kuttan was about to occupy. It had only a bed, a table and a chair.

"I am going out. Do you need anything?" Maya asked as Kuttan was settling down in his room.

"No. Thank you," Kuttan replied and moved towards the balcony. He heard the door locked behind him. He looked from the balcony towards the speeding vehicles on the over-bridge. He saw them coughing smoke out and spreading a sheet of dust around them.

A group of children were playing cricket at the ground behind the boundary walls of the apartments. He looked at them carefully. They were skinny, scantily dressed yet jubilant without any worries. He was one such boy many years ago struggling to survive every day but had lesser fears and doubts. He had worked extremely hard to climb past the wall and to stand here in the balcony of a posh residential building, yet was not sure of what he wanted from his life.

Kuttan realised that may be he had reached far ahead in life. First time he dared to ask himself, *"What do I want from life? What's the purpose of all the struggle that I had been through? Is Maya the destination that I had strived for or having a destination is a Maya?"*

***

Chapter 26

The Trunk and the Secrets

"Dileep! What's in this trunk?" Maya asked Kuttan as she played with the old iron lock on the trunk.

"My old stuff, my savings… pretty much my life till we met. I inherited it from my father. I mean the trunk," Kuttan said patting on the trunk pushing out a deep breathe of guilt and regret.

"I want to see. Please. May I open it?" Maya looked at Kuttan with her lined black eyes begging and directing him to open the trunk, both at the same time.

Kuttan had avoided showing it to anyone until then. But the manner in which Maya cajoled him, he could not resist. He needed to reciprocate the trust she had shown in him with the secret place even against the wish of Mats. Moreover, she was rich and didn't need to eye his savings, his cautious mind agreed with his naïve heart.

"Wow! It feels as if I have discovered some treasure on a treasure hunt. Like this trunk would be full of gold coins, jewels and lots of money," Maya joked. She was visibly excited.

"I am not sure about gold but there might be a hidden treasure within, you never know," Kuttan replied with a smile that had hidden secrets underneath.

Maya opened the trunk. There were a few old clothes, some were torn but neatly folded and packed. Underneath the clothes was an old black and white framed photo. Kuttan's parents were sitting and he was in his mother's lap. Mother was wearing a sari. She had long hair, wide large eyes and refused to smile. She looked gorgeous. His father was a thin dark man with trimmed beard and moustache. He wore a South Indian dhoti and shirt. The child was the only one laughing whole heartedly enjoying worriless the protective cover and love of his parents.

"Hey! Your parents? Oh...your mother is so beautiful. Where are they?"

"My father died when I was four. Mother is there in my village, happily married to a land lord, spending a luxurious life," Kuttan replied as if forwarding an accusation.

"I am so sorry about your father. You never mentioned about your mother?"

"There is nothing worth mentioning about her. I don't like talking about her," Kuttan shot back without looking at the photo.

"That's mean. I too have differences with my mother but does not mean I stop talking to her. Mothers always do things to protect their children and their wellbeing. We may not understand the reasoning behind everything they do but surely all mothers do love their children."

Although Maya was not sure if she believed everything she said but disapproved Kuttan's tone of introduction of his mother.

"Huff...All mothers don't," Kuttan had his eyes filled just when he controlled his emotion and said, "Let me show you my secret."

There was a thin wooden board covering the base which made the voluptuous trunk to seem smaller. The board was covered with a white cotton cloth. Kuttan removed the cloth and lifted the board. There were four packets wrapped with clothes. Maya opened the packets to her astonishment, all the packets had money. A two rupee note was kept separate laminated in a transparent plastic cover.

"So much of money in this old trunk! How much is this?" Maya's eyes almost propped up.

"Ha-ha... relax. This is my hard earned money. All of the eight lakh ninety six thousand five hundred and two rupees, every single paisa of it. I have worked for twenty two years, ever since I was six," Kuttan didn't realise that he was proud of himself and probably valued it so much.

"Wow! I knew you were working and you had money. But, this was beyond my imagination."

"How did you know?" The question came to Kuttan casually.

"Of course you told me. How would I know else? You had told me about the kind of part time jobs you used to do as a student. So I guessed you must be having savings," Maya cleared the air, "Why don't you put it in bank?"

"I had always kept it with me. It gives me a sense of protection. I have seen the meanest form of this world; the only thing that matters here is money."

"I disagree. I chose you knowing that you were an ordinary guy. I didn't know you had savings of this kind, still I love you. If it was for money then definitely I would not have chosen you. I like your inherent qualities," Maya didn't hesitate to put her point of view.

"You are one of those few pleasant exceptions that I have seen," Kuttan said apologetically, "Now it's your turn. I want to see what is there in your almirah."

"Nothing special. Just regular women stuff."

"I have never seen these 'women stuff', so please," Kuttan tried the trick that she had used on him but execution needed the cajoling effect of the depth of her mesmerising eyes, which he lacked. The effort failed.

"Aha…nice clever move, you fox! Its bad manners. No way am I going to show you my private stuff, not yet," Maya pinched Kuttan over his cheeks and moved out of the room.

"That's so unfair. Looking in to a guy's trunk, if it's not bad manners then how come looking in to a girl's personal stuff could be? I have just shown you my life's most important secret," Kuttan protested.

"I have already shown a big secret. Forgot?" Maya turned around momentarily and teased him, "Bring me a new secret, then we shall think."

Kuttan traced, with his eyes, the outline of her body flowing rhythmically, outpouring the excessive charm of her curves through the shorts and t-shirt. The beauty made him forget the protest, he followed her.

"Wait. Don't come inside until I tell you to," Maya playfully commanded.

Kuttan waited outside her room. Kuttan loved it when Maya took command in their relation; she was good at it. With each passing day Kuttan had become more addicted to her. He looked up to her for love, support, suggestions, joy and care. The only wish which she did not fulfil yet was to have sex. He was still a virgin. Maya somehow was not ready to have sex with him, she seemed to enjoy the companionship more than anything else in the relationship, and he was ready to wait until she was ready.

Kuttan was lost in his thoughts when he heard Maya shouting from inside asking him to get in. He slowly opened the door and found that the lights were switched off, only the dim light was lit. The room had been cooled to the minimum temperature. Maya laid on the bed covered in white soft furred blanket.

"Close the door and get in to the blanket," Maya looked at Kuttan with a suggestive smile. When Kuttan was about to enter, "No, I mean naked."

"Are you?" Kuttan's eyes propped up.

"Shh... do as I say," Maya gestured by slowly putting index finger over her pink everted lips.

Kuttan didn't ask any further questions. He undressed himself and went into the blanket. She pulled him closer to her. She was naked too, she felt softer than the blanket. He could feel the warmth of her body underneath the warm blanket comforting from the cold outside. She took his hands and moved it all over her body slowly and said, "I think am ready to offer you all my secrets. Here's my secret place, feel it," she made him touch her clitoris and then feel inside the vagina.

A rush of blood pumped through the blood vessels in his body, making him the warmest and the most aroused he had ever been. He jumped on to her. They kissed passionately. She took his penis in her hands, it was hard and ready to obey her command. She guided him in to her. They made love unless they both could not have had any further.

Kuttan was not a virgin anymore. He felt wonderful.

"This was my first time," Kuttan still had a warm blood flushed face.

"Hmm… I know," Maya didn't open her eyes. She was still lost in the moment.

"How do you know?"

"Hmmm… I know," she teased him.

"Was this your first time?" Kuttan kept staring at her face.

"No, and no more questions. Don't spoil the mood," she pulled him towards her and held him close to her bosom.

Kuttan knew he should not have asked the question; he felt jealous of the man who had the pleasure of the wonderful feeling with her before him. He knew the answer very well but hoped that she would lie to him, but she was too honestly in love with him, which reinforced that now she belonged to him; only to him.

At the second thought he held her tight and kissed her. They felt aroused again. Succumbing further to the deeper desires they made love to each other passionately, again.

Chapter 27

The Pseudo-protection

"I have got something to tell you, something I have not discussed with anyone yet," Kuttan started hesitantly when they were having breakfast next day morning, in the balcony. It was a bright Sunday morning.

"Hmm... tell me, what is it?" Maya asked as she took a bite on the cheese sandwich that Kuttan had specially prepared for her; she liked salty cheese.

"Please be honest about what you think."

"I will try. Let me first hear it."

"I have a dream of becoming a successful rich businessman. I wish to own a big company, big means real big. But..." Kuttan started hesitantly but, later his eyes glistened as he spoke the words. But... what he lacked was self-belief, so he needed someone else's approval. Someone who was close to him, who understood him, and whom he could trust blindly. Sometimes it takes a life time to find one such person, sometimes they are right in front of your eyes but you fail to identify them.

"It's extremely difficult if not impossible. But if anyone whom I know has the capability of making it that big, it's you. You have fought all your life against the odds and still never gave up. That's exactly what is needed to be successful anywhere. What business are you planning?"

"I am thinking of an IT start up. I think I can do it with few colleagues at the office," Kuttan sounded doubtful.

"Do you have such good friends in office? I don't think you should take that risk. It would need lots of investment. Also, you need contacts, or else who would give you projects?"

"Hmm..." Kuttan was dejected.

"Let me see if I can help you. My brother has the contacts needed but would he help you is a million dollar question."

"Why?"

"He needs everything to be under his control. So letting you have access to his contacts without having anything in return won't appeal to him," she paused for a moment and then continued, "But if I am involved in this project then he will become interested, at least my mom would. I have been their head ache always. I was never interested in their business. So, if I say I am a partner in this they would definitely help us."

"But you said you were not interested in business?"

"I am not. Only to make him help you I would become a partner. Then when you start to do well by self, you can buy my share and do away with the partnership."

"Why would I do so? I wish you to be my partner forever," Kuttan stressed on the 'forever'.

"Because that's not my dream. By the way, I meant to do away with only the business partnership," Maya teased Kuttan as she collected the finished plates and went to kitchen. On the way she stopped and came back. She kissed Kuttan softly and said, "Don't worry we can make it happen."

Kuttan smiled. He was satisfied, he had found his partner for his life. He followed her to kitchen.

"What's your dream?"

"Don't you know?" Maya hated it whenever Kuttan asked formal questions for just the sake of asking something in reciprocal.

"Fashion designing. But you are studying MBA, aren't you?"

"Nope. Not exactly. After UG course in computer science, I have done a diploma in fashion designing and boutique management. I started working on a project recently, thanks to your motivation."

"You never told me?" Kuttan sounded little disappointed.

"No one outside my college circle knows. I wished to tell you but the topic never came up. My family thinks I am doing MBA. Since both colleges are under same management and I had struck a deal with the administrator. I have managed to befool them so far. I can't risk my brother knowing about it."

"So that's why you don't go out partying and merry around with friends other than me," Kuttan probably for the first time realised that he was a compromised choice she had made for the sake of her ambition, "Is this why you want to be my start up partner? So that your brother won't bother you and you could more freely enjoy the course you are passionate about."

"No, that's not the only reason. I wish to help you in whatever way I can. Actually, I wish to go to Paris. There is a scholarship program of one and half years in Fashion designing at International Fashion Academy. I had applied for it. They have asked me to submit a project. The project, application and fees everything will cost me about ten to fifteen lakhs. But I don't have the money. So kind of stuck with it. I know exactly how it feels to not be able to follow one's passion. That's why I wish to help you," Maya was no more cheerful, she explained calmly.

"Why don't you ask your family for help?"

"Are you serious? What did I tell you about my family?" Maya got irritated.

"I mean you need not tell them about this but something else, say you need a car?" Kuttan tried to simplify the problem.

"What do you think? Am I stupid? If this was so simple I would have got it done a long back. They never transfer bulk amount to my account. They pay for all my expenses directly. All I get is monthly twenty thousand as pocket money. Can you imagine? I am twenty five, still on pocket money," Maya was filled with self-pity.

"Twenty thousand after all expenses. You could have actually saved a lot," Kuttan unintentionally sounded judgemental.

"Hmm... I just could not. That's why I envy you so much. I wish I could too," now Maya was looking for some assurance, a probable helping hand.

"I wish I could help you. But you know my start up would require much more than what I have in my hands right now," Kuttan expressed his helplessness in a rather heartless tone. To part with his life time savings was the most painful thing he could think of, until then. He was enslaved to the illusion of pseudo-protection it offered.

"I know. I didn't expect any help of that sort from you either. All I need from you is a companion. I feel so lonely at times."

"I know how it feels to be lonely when you have people who should have taken care of you, but failed to do so." Did he mean the words? His words failed to match his actions.

Kuttan held her tight to his chest. Maya hid in to his chest. His hug was comforting. Kuttan looked out through the kitchen window. He knew he had let her down but she graciously managed not to embarrass him. A crow sat on the window panel pierced in to Kuttan's gaze; it seemed to disapprove Kuttan, or was it just his conscience reflecting in its eyes? He looked away in to the distant blank blue sky wondering what else he could have said.

Chapter 28

Shubhasya shigram

"I have a good news and a bad news for you, which one would you like to hear first?" Maya was in joyful mood.

"Hmm…I guess both the news together," Kuttan answered after a moment of thought.

"I cancelled my application for scholarship at IFA in Paris and my brother would help us only if we become partner in 'his' IT start-up," the fake joy wandered away, swept by the lips spread in despair.

"Where is the good news?" Kuttan sounded confused.

"My application one, I thought that's a good news for you. Now you need not feel guilty about not helping me," Maya sounded mysteriously calm for such an accusation.

Kuttan realised a big truth- women don't forget they just pretend, once let down they might not show it then but later somehow will let you know of their disapproval.

"I would have helped you. Believe me! But I have to start a business with limited resources. I hope you understand," Kuttan felt bad but was far from being apologetic.

"Relax Dileep. I was joking. Either we can accept my brother's offer, once we have our own contacts and projects we can break up partnership with him and start our own or I have another plan for you, a bit more risky."

"What's the next plan?" Kuttan asked without a second thought.

"I have a friend in a private bank, actually a friend's friend. He is chief manager there. He can help us get a business loan sanctioned. But for that you would have to open an account there and deposit the amount you have. I would present you as my partner, which may make things easy."

"This idea sounds better but still I am not sure. I mean I have never dealt with banks."

"Then how do you expect to raise money? You don't have any other investors, these are the only ways possible as far as I could think. I have given you options, rest you decide," Maya sounded very clear in her mind with the plan.

"I didn't mean to offend you."

"Do you know what your problem is? You are always too afraid to take risk. Otherwise with the kind of hard working focussed nature of yours, you could scale any heights. Look around, anyone who is successful has taken risk at some point of time. Now is your time Dileep. You have to move out of this comfort zone of pseudo-protection," Maya desperately wanted Kuttan to take chance, "The money that you think is your protection is actually the chain across your soul that is restricting you from taking leaps towards your goal."

"I think... I need some time to think again," Kuttan said more to himself. He felt something inside pulling him backwards.

"Okay. But remember the more you think the lesser the chance that you would take the risk. The lesser the chance of risk, even lesser would be the chance that you would ever become a successful entrepreneur, the kind of you have dreamt of. Opportunities don't come too often, you have to grab them when they come," with that Maya closed the conversation.

To let go the money away from him was a huge psychological blockade that had grown with him since childhood. Maya realised it. She was probably the only person who could persuade him to believe and invest in his dream. Maya left, leaving behind Kuttan to think.

Kuttan took a day off and thought about the proposal. He

realised that he had to trust people if he had to do something in life and who else could have been a better person to start with, than Maya. Maya had offered to help him without any personal gain even after Kuttan had disappointed her. She had supported him always and if she believed in the idea, it must be good.

"I have thought about it and I think you are right. My obsession with saving is taking the essence out of my life. It's holding me back. To be able to realise my dream, the first thing I have to do is to re-move this mental blockade, as you had said," Kuttan said as soon as Maya returned to the flat.

"I knew you would take the right decision," Maya replied as she gulped water from the bottle that she took out from the fridge.

"How did you know?" Kuttan asked innocently.

"Because you are an intelligent brave man. I am so proud of you," Maya pinched Kuttan on his cheeks and continued, "You have always faced challenges the life had thrown at you, face on. You are made for big things in life; I know it, even more than you do."

"Your support and enthusiasm is so contagious. Thank you Maya," Kuttan looked straight in to her eyes and moved closer to-wards her, "Thank you for the support, thank you for the belief you have in me, thank you for loving me, thank you for making me feel I am worth your love..." before he could embarrass her more, she kissed him, "I love you. I want to spend the rest of my life with you. Do you?" Kuttan asked still looking at her as if he was holding his most prized possession.

"I do, but not now. Not before both of us achieve our dreams," Maya kissed him softly.

"But you cancelled the application?" Kuttan felt bad as he said those words.

"That's temporary. I have submitted my project proposal and if they like I can do it later, may be next year. For now, our focus must be on your start up," Maya tried to console Kuttan and self.

"You mean our start up," Kuttan corrected her, "So when shall we go to the bank?"

"Tomorrow. *Shubhasya shigram* (auspicious things must be

done at the earliest)," Maya winked at Kuttan as he stood amazed at her positive attitude.

"You are such an amazing woman. I love you so much," Kuttan held her tight.

Chapter 29

The Phone Call

Next day Kuttan and Maya went to the bank to see the manager Aarush Mishra, a well-built dark man in his late thirties. After finishing the formalities for opening the account they sat in his cabin for about twenty minutes discussing the project.

"There are so many start-ups these days, we are not even sure which one is going to click and which one is going to fail," Aarush tried to sound funny but sounded rather arrogant.

"No one could know unless we start. And moreover it's the attitude of the team leader that decides the fate of the company," Maya was not impressed.

"Can't agree more with you. Hope you have such a leader and team," Aarush replied cautiously as he was not sure about the profile of people he was dealing with. All he knew was that Maya was from an influential business family.

"Of course we have. This gentle man is the leader and no one could be more focussed than he is. Also, we can get help from my brother, he is also in to computer business. You know him. Don't you?"

"Oh yes, that sounds wonderful. Then the loan should not be a problem. But our leader doesn't seem to be involved in this conversation," Aarush looked at Kuttan and said.

"There is no point in bragging about what I can do. I would like you to see the result," Kuttan tried to sound positive but ended up sounding ignorant.

"That's not how it is sir. You have to submit a detailed project, based on that we could sanction loan; subject to approval from higher office, which I can manage. But we would need a guarantor and a property as security. If your brother can be a guarantor?"

"I can be the guarantor that is pretty much the same. The property papers we will provide later. You can trust us. Can't you?" Maya was at her persuasive best.

"I think I can," Aarush agreed, "In that case it won't be much of a problem."

"Thank you so much," both said simultaneously.

"Don't forget about the property papers, that's important."

"Sure. Thank you so much," Maya said when Kuttan's phone rang, screen read, *'xxxxxx756 calling...'*

"You can attend the call, it's no problem," Aarush told politely.

"No need. It's not important," Kuttan replied rather rudely that created a moment of uncomfortable silence in otherwise cordial conversation. Realising the awkwardness Maya stepped in.

"We would leave now. Once again Aarush you are such a nice guy, even better than what Roshan had told me."

"Oh it's my job," Aarush swelled with pride while pretending it to be a usual affair.

"Bye. See you."

"Have a nice day."

Kuttan didn't say good bye. He seemed disturbed.

"You should be a little polite when you need to get a favour from someone," Maya sounded disappointed at his attitude as they came out of the building.

"Hmmm..."

"What happened? Whose call was that? You seem disturbed," Maya predicted the reason for sudden change in his mood.

"My mother's husband," Kuttan's facial muscles strained as he chewed at nothing.

"Means your father?" Maya was puzzled as she knew his father was dead.

"No. My step-father," Kuttan spit on the road as he mentioned his relation.

"That was disgusting," Maya frowned.

"So is he..." Kuttan said and walked ahead.

"Why didn't you attend the call?"

"I didn't want to talk to him. He reminds me of everything that I wish to forget."

"Then how do you know his number? You must call back, it could be something important."

"If it's that important, he will call again."

"He has called you for the first time in so many years. Don't you think that is some sort of a sign?"

"No."

Again the phone rang. Screen read, *'xxxxxxx756 calling...'* Maya went near Kuttan, held his hand and said, "Dileep attend the call. Don't be afraid, just attend."

Kuttan held Maya's hand tightly, and attended the phone call.

"Hello! Hmm... Hmm... Hmm... I am not sure, shall see if I can," Kuttan disconnected the call in less than a minute and looked in front of him as if he was staring at his past.

"What did he say?" Maya asked as they hired a taxi.

"Nothing important," Kuttan sat beside her.

"What was it Dileep?" Maya commanded.

"My mother is sick, had been for the past few years. She may survive only a few more days. She wish to see me," Kuttan tried to control his emotions but his shivering voice betrayed him.

"To this you said, you are not sure! You are going, I am damn sure," Maya too got emotional, "You can't be mad at her for so long. She was in love. So are you now. You must understand the desire to be loved by someone, to be cared by someone."

"But she was my mother," Kuttan struggled not to cry.

"So what. She was a human being too. She didn't leave you,

you left her. Don't do this to yourself. You won't be able to survive the regret and guilt," Maya tried to console him. She pulled his head in to her lap. Kuttan sobbed without any resistance.

***

Maya drove Kuttan to the railway station three days after the phone call. The train was delayed by two hours so they went to a nearby pub. Maya ordered red wine so did Kuttan.

"The bill is on me," Kuttan said as soon as they placed the order.

"Are you sure?" Maya was amazed at this sudden change in his attitude.

"Thanks to you, now I realise that there are more important things in life than money. Money has its value only when it's spent," Kuttan leaned back on his chair.

"I am impressed yet again," Maya raised the glass of wine, "For the new Chapter in your life."

"Our life," Kuttan corrected her, "Keep these you may need some money as you look for new office space and apartment for us. I feel bad that you need to do this alone," Kuttan placed a signed blank cheque on the table.

"We can do it after you come back. The loan will also get sanctioned by then."

"No. We need not delay this. Moreover, I am not sure how long would I have to be there," Kuttan waived to the waiter to refill the glasses.

"I shall go to visit my mother to get the Kollur estate property papers any time in between. She must help us."

"I will miss you," drunk Kuttan was far more romantic than the sober one.

"Hurry! Or you will miss the train as well," Maya teased him as the wine made them laugh louder than they intended.

***

"Sir! Please pay the bill. It is closing time," said the waiter.

"Hmm... yes sure."

The dim light in the pub had been replaced by bright white lights. The music was shut down. The college students, after having a wonderful time, were pulling themselves out of the place. The waiters and the cleaning staff were at their super-fast best. Kuttan paid the bill and left a fifty rupee note as tip. He tried Maya's number once again which was still not reachable. Worried, he left.

Chapter 30

The Search

Kuttan went to Maya's college to enquire about her ab
sence. He reached the college in the evening after the
classes were over and small groups of young future entrepreneurs, fashion enthusiasts, scientists, economists were all busy
enjoying the relaxed evening. He asked a few students about Maya,
but didn't get any response from them.

Finally, a guy identified Maya when he saw her photo in Kuttan's
mobile, "Oh Yes! I know her. She is an alumni of our college, she was
my senior. She finished her diploma last year. Still she visits the college sometimes, I have seen her couple of weeks back. You can ask
Shiksha, I had seen them together."

"Where can I find Shiksha?" Kuttan asked, not sure what to
expect.

"She must be in the canteen, I will show you."

Kuttan followed the guy who moved rather slowly for his comfort waving, chatting and greeting every leaf and stone on the way to
the canteen.

"There she is, the one in red shirt," the guy pointed from the
entrance towards a very fair plump girl who seemed to talk to her
colleagues rather animatedly.

Kuttan went close the table where the group of five students were sitting, "Excuse me! Shiksha?"

"Yes Sir. How can I enlighten you?" She laughed loudly as if she had just cracked a joke. Kuttan was not in a mood to appreciate any joke, leave a substandard one. "I am Shiksha," she repeated, with raised brows and shake of head, to Kuttan who seemed baffled at the reply.

"Hi, I am Dileep, Maya's friend. May I speak to you for a moment, I mean in person?" Kuttan spoke in a low polite voice.

"Hmm… ok! Why just for a moment? We can talk for long time but every half an hour I will charge you a cool drink and snack," she was about to laugh again when she noted the worried expression on his face, "Relax! It was a joke. Tell me what is it? Excuse us guys."

They moved to a vacant seat in the corner.

"Do you know where Maya is now? I have no idea about her whereabouts for the past three weeks. Her phone is not reachable as well. Did she come here in the past three weeks?" Kuttan started the conversation.

"Yes she was here two weeks back. The scholarship project she was working on, hope you know about it," Kuttan moved his head in affirmation, "it got approved by the IFA. She came here to get a letter of recommendation from the college principal."

"I thought that she had cancelled the application."

"Actually she had, but they liked the idea very much so they provided her fifty percent rebate in the fees. Lucky girl, she desperately wanted the scholarship. She had worked very hard for the past one year, after finishing her diploma, but didn't have support from the family. Some friend of hers had motivated and helped her, she had once told," Shiksha casually replied while taking a bite of her burger.

"When was she supposed to join there? Did she tell you something?"

"Hmm… No idea. She didn't tell," she took another bite, "Is everything all right?" She asked as she looked at Kuttan's worried face.

"No! Actually yes…nothing serious; just that I was not able to locate her, so enquired. Thank you," Kuttan mumbled in a hurried voice while trying to fake a relaxed smile.

Kuttan paid for the snacks.

"Are you the friend who helped her?" Shiksha asked as Kuttan was leaving.

"Nope. I am the friend who failed to help her, I guess," Kuttan was disappointed at something, probably at the fact that he could not understand her passion for fashion designing even after she had told him or may be because she didn't feel important to tell him about her success. He sighed and left.

***

"Hi Aarush! Can you spare me a couple of minutes?" Kuttan knocked and partially opened the door of the chief manager's cabin at the bank.

"Hey Dileep! I was about to call you, please come in. Your loan is not yet sanctioned. Maya did not submit the papers, yet. I had told her that we need your signature at few more places as well," Aarush placed a few documents with small cross marked at the places where signatures were needed.

"Did Maya come here in past couple of weeks?" Kuttan signed the papers.

"Yes, once. She came to clear a cheque, I remember. That day she had told me she was going to get papers soon but since then there was no news about both of you, so I was about to call you," he replied as he went through the signed documents.

"How much money did she withdraw?"

"Let me check," Aarush peeked in to his computer screen, "Eight lakhs."

"Ok. Thank you Aarush," Kuttan said after a brief pause.

"You were here to ask about something. Weren't you?"

"Nothing," Kuttan answered and left the cabin failing to say good bye again.

The clouds of doubts that had accumulated in his head were getting darker and darker, day by day. First time he had trusted someone more than anyone, probably himself; he now doubted the trust.

He had many questions in his mind, *"Where is Maya? Why her phone is not reachable? Why would she not tell me about the acceptance of her scholarship project? Why didn't she submit the property papers? Did she leave for Paris? Did she love me? Did she betray my trust? How could she do this to me?"*

The severity of doubts kept creeping in the order. The more he thought about her, the more those doubts invaded his sanity. He needed someone to talk to calm himself down so that he could stop having these non-sense thoughts in his mind.

He thought of Gowri.

Chapter 31

The End of a Platonic Relationship

Next day was a Sunday. Kuttan met Gowri at a cafeteria near her apartment. He reached there one hour before time, he didn't wish to stay alone in the flat. By the time when she reached the café, Kuttan had already finished two coffees and ordered for a third one.

"Hi Dileep. Seems like someone has already started enjoyment without waiting for an old friend," Gowri commented looking at the table as she took her seat.

"Hi Gowri," Kuttan wished to smile but failed to act, he was tired of pretending everything was all right.

"What happened? Why so serious? Any problem?" Now Gowri too had a serious face.

"Nothing serious, just wanted to see you, felt like talking to you."

"Just? First time in almost one year, hard to believe. You can tell me whatever it is. I am your same old friend," Gowri placed her right arm over his left arm on the table.

Kuttan kept looking at the steam coming out of the coffee cup (the third one) on the table. The silence prevailed for few more minutes. Then Kuttan spoke without any preamble, "Maya seems to be missing. Can neither locate her nor contact her. I am getting worried."

He had wished to talk anything other than Maya, rather ended up speaking about her at the first instance.

"Are you worried for her or for yourself?" Gowri knew Kuttan very well, "I mean are you worried for her safety or are you worried that she had left you?"

"Both," Kuttan could not look in to her eyes. He felt ashamed for no reason.

"Don't lie. You are worried that she had unceremoniously dumped you. You have not changed. Have you?" Bitterness in her words reflected their bitter past experience.

"What did she say when she met you that day?" Kuttan didn't want to carry over an argument from the past. Also, he didn't feel like giving her an explanation.

"Told you, nothing important. She was on her way to see some travel agent. She said she was going to visit her mother."

"Why was she going to visit her mother, did she tell you?"

"No, actually I didn't ask. It was none of my business."

"Which travel agent?"

"I think it was Exquisite travels, near the railway station."

"Waiter! Please bring the bill. Sorry have to leave now," Kuttan responded drastically.

"What's the matter? Why are you so disturbed? Is everything all right?"

"I don't know but shall know soon," Kuttan said drooping his shoulders.

As the waiter kept the bill on table, Kuttan took it and paid.

"I was wrong. Maybe you have changed, for good, I would be-lieve," Gowri said with a pleasant smile.

Kuttan didn't pay heed to her compliment and moved out of the café swiftly. She sat there for some more time, with her cup of coffee, after Kuttan had left. She didn't let him know but she was worried for him. She sighed, remembering the argument they had before they broke up which seemed to have happened in the last century. Gowri still doubted Kuttan's version of the story.

***

"All women are the same. They are selfish like cats, whoever would feed them more milk they would sit in their lap and offer the comfort of their cushion; you know what I mean. Gowri is no different, she will dump you the moment she would find someone better," Surya vulgarly enacted trying to provoke Kuttan. He was trying to convince that short term relations with benefits were better- more pleasure and less hurt.

"You have seen only such girls because you are so. You don't know anything about Gowri," Kuttan rubbished Surya.

"I know her quite well now. We are close, very close; closer than you expect," Surya squeezed Kuttan's shoulder.

"You bastard! Stay away from her," Kuttan held Surya by his collar.

"Ask her if you dare, you pussy!" Surya punched him in lower abdomen and left. Kuttan lay on the floor moaning in pain.

Kuttan waited for few weeks. He pretended as if the fight had never happened between them. Surya, one evening, as usual brought one of his girl-friends to the internet café. Kuttan had hidden a camera in their cabin. He recorded Surya's vulnerability with his girlfriend. He could not wait to show it to Gowri who probably didn't exactly understand what happened behind the close door of the cabin. She would be thankful to him for saving her from Surya's dirty tricks, he had thought.

Kuttan went to Gowri who was sitting alone in the class room at the back corner bench, "I have got something to show you. Be ready for the surprise or rather shock," he was too excited at the thought of the love and appreciation she was above to endow upon him.

"What the hell is this? What the hell do you think I am? I had told you I knew it and I was not interested," Gowri boiled over as Kuttan showed her the 'surprise' without any explanation.

"I thought you would be grateful to me," Kuttan didn't expect such a reaction from her. He was shocked and extremely disappointed.

"For what? I don't care what he does in his private life; we have had these discussions in the past so many times. Don't you get it? Are you stupid or what?" Gowri could not control her disappointment too.

"But then I didn't have any evidence," Kuttan pointed towards the mobile phone.

"Delete it now. No one else should come to know about this. Do you understand?" The disgust was obvious in her voice.

Kuttan deleted it.

"Why are you so upset? You didn't like the video or is it because it had 'your' Surya enjoying with another girl?" Kuttan stared at her with a kind of aggression she had never seen from him. His eyes were reddened and the voice shivered.

"What?" Gowri could not believe what she was hearing.

"Don't act innocent. I do understand what is going on here. I am NOT stupid. You are bored with me, you have got 'the better' one. So now you can dump me. He was right, you are closer to him, closer than you are to me. You both are fooling me. Aren't you? Did you sleep with him?"

"You are such a hopeless creep. You pervert! You don't own me. I can do whatever I want to. Do you understand? I have never said that I love you. I liked you very much, you were my best friend, but now I even doubt that," tears rolled out of her eyes spontaneously. She was hurt, she had loved him very much but never admitted it. Each of his words pierced through her.

"So what was that night at the ashram, you whore?" Kuttan yelled.

"That was a mistake, I guess. No I know, that was a big mistake," Gowri ran past him sobbing.

Kuttan had apologised afterwards, many times. They became friends again. Kuttan hoped to win back her affection. The broken pieces were joined, they pretended everything to be normal but deep inside they both knew the cracks had become too obvious to be completely sealed. The affection she had was lost. Their platonic relationship was never the same.

Chapter 32

The Beggar Saint

When Kuttan reached outside the office of the 'Exquisite Travels' in the evening, it was closed. He tried the number on the advertisement billboard but there was no response. Kuttan tried several times but all the calls went unanswered.

Undecided, he roamed through the busy streets. He didn't want to go back to the apartment; he didn't want to go to any place that would remind him of Maya. He roamed without any destination to avoid any thought about her; the irony was that wherever he went, thought of the time spent with her filled every vacuum of his thoughts.

Late night, when the city finally cradled to silent sleep, Kuttan sat on the footpath in front of the travel office. A group of beggars who had lit fire in a corner invited him to join them. Kuttan first resisted but later the temptation of the comfort of fire in a relatively cold night attracted him.

"What are you doing here, you seem to be from a respectable family?" an old man with overgrown beard and filthy dressing predicted looking at decently dressed Kuttan.

"Haha…," Kuttan laughed aloud, a soulless laugh which resonated in his ear, "I am neither respectable nor do I have a family."

"Then you can join us, we don't have any membership charges

like your posh clubs," taunted a young man. The whole group laughed unanimously.

"Hmm. You are all so lucky to have each other. I should have been somewhere in a group like yours but..." Kuttan said in a low voice which no one seemed to notice, they were all busy boozing after a day's 'hard work'.

"Without a family? You must have worked really hard to achieve whatever you might have. In that case what's the reason for this sadness? You should be proud of yourself," only the old man was interested in his conversation. He had a face similar to the chief saint at the Ashram, Swami Satchitananda.

"I have not achieved anything to be proud of."

"Are you sure? Definitely you must have. You are sad at losing something, means you were good enough to have it in first place. If you had something once, you can have it again; if you had achieved something in your life, however small, you can achieve something better and bigger again. But, do you believe it? Remember son all the answers to your queries and miseries lie within you, in your past. You just have to look back and think where you went wrong. Don't forget the path that had lead you this far."

Kuttan didn't seem interested in any positive talks. The cheap rum they offered had begun its effect, he slipped in to sleep.

Next morning warm gentle breeze woke up Kuttan. He woke up to his dismay, a stray dog was sniffing him. Kuttan shooed away the dog and looked around, all were gone. No one was around, not even any evidence of fire lit last night was seen. He had a bad headache. He pressed his forehead and vigorously moved fingers through hairs. He could not make out if the man with whom he had conversation last night was for real or was it just a hallucination?

Kuttan went to public toilet near the railway station to fresh up as the day had begun in the busy city. He looked at his blurred self in the rusted mirror, *"Was it a dream or was it real? Had I seen a beggar or was it the chief saint from the ashram? Have I achieved something in life? Does the problem lie within me? How can one look back in to his past?"* Suddenly he took off the eyes from the mirror. He did not dare

138

look back in to his past. It was too much of pain there. For the first time in life, during the search, he had begun to realise that people around him didn't see him as a lowly life, but it was himself. He was not dependent on the people around for his life, but himself.

For convenience and out of habit of self-pity, Kuttan refused to look in to the mirror, and in to his past.

***

"Hello sir*ji*! How can I help you?" asked an extremely polite bald big fat man with French beard at the travels.

"I wish to enquire about travel to Paris?" Kuttan hesitated, not knowing where to start.

"When are you planning to travel sir? We can book you tickets as well as do all the paper work needed for traveling."

"Do you arrange for student visas also?"

"Anything sir. You just tell and it will be done."

"Did you arrange a travel for a woman, Maya, in the past one or two weeks to Paris?"

"Maya? Hmm... don't know sir. So many people come daily and Paris is such common destination for us," he bragged.

Kuttan showed him the photo in his mobile. He didn't smile, instead looked straight in to his eyes.

"Are you from police? Is there some trouble for me?" he frowned with sweat over his bald head.

"No! She is my friend and I can't locate her. Just a casual en-quiry," Kuttan didn't wish to acknowledge, to a stranger, that he was seeking his help to know about his girlfriend.

"Yes she had come two weeks back. I had arranged for her travel to Paris," the man was relieved to hear that.

"Did she book return tickets?" Kuttan asked cautiously as if he knew the answer.

"Let me check," he looked in to his computer, "No, she didn't book. Oh yes now I remember, I had insisted but she said she was not sure when she would return. She had said that she would book the tickets later."

Kuttan didn't ask any more questions. He didn't wish to. He

left without saying a word, he didn't hear the voice of the man from behind. He just moved out and started walking purposelessly towards his implicit destination, the doom.

***

He came running into their apartment which was no longer 'theirs'. He didn't take the lift; he climbed seven storeys to reach the flat on the eighth floor. He wanted to suffer. He fell and bruised on the way but didn't feel the pain. He was short of breath, his heart beating out of chest. These were trivial when compared to what was going within him.

He stumbled upon nothing as he reached towards the door of the apartment. The key fell off his hands on to the imported tiles flooring the veranda of the posh society where he was living; where he would not have dared to even peek into if it was not for her.

He opened the door and entered the apartment's drawing room. The apartment was no longer well-furnished as it was couple of weeks back, before she had left. His personal stuff accounted for only ten percentage of the furnishing. The remaining were hers, most of which was missing now.

He roamed in the apartment again and again, like a crazy who had lost his shadow, and was searching for it. He searched in all the rooms hoping to find her somewhere. *'May be she was hiding somewhere. May be she was playing a prank on him,'* he hoped, he prayed, and yet he knew it was false. He could not find her anywhere. After what he had learnt about her over the past one week though, he was 'almost' sure, that she was gone forever and would never return.

As if the previous several attempts of his to find her in the vast city over past one week were not enough, his heart wished to make sure one more time 'in case if'.

She was gone. With her was gone his desire to live. He had lost everything that he had, loved, possessed and believed to be his, in a matter of few weeks. It wasn't even 3 weeks since his mother parted the world. And now he stands here alone. Very alone, losing love of his life and all his entire life's savings.

Everything was just an illusion, *a Maya*. He didn't feel like living in this world anymore. This world has ill-treated him enough. He decided to put an end to it one last time.

Was he a coward? No, he was a fighter. He had always been a fighter. Since childhood he had fought against his main opponent, 'his fate', with great zeal to reach where he was now. Where he was now? He himself had never realised or appreciated. God, if there were any, and life had been unfair to him. His miseries and efforts never matched what he had achieved in his life. He had two choices-he could either continue fighting or could altogether quit. The decision was his to make and he didn't want his destiny to decide on it. He had decided. The decision was not 'just' because a girl had left him but an accumulation of all the pain until then. It was his way to show the middle finger to this audacious world, the destiny, the non-existing God and Ramesh; to tell them that they had been impudent to him.

Tomorrow is his birthday. He would end his life on the very day when it all started at 12:00 AM.

He pressed the power button and his phone beeped to life, it showed 8:55 PM. Let this mobile gifted by her, his first smart phone, guide this ignorant, uncouth, not-so-smart creature through the countdown of his life. He sat on the wooden chair. He decided to write a note or may be a letter, not to blame anyone but let out his agony that had become unbearable. Then, he would cry out loud and jump of the balcony exactly at 12:00 AM. Everything was planned but then, his plans had never worked before.

***

~~Dear~~ God,

I do not know why I am addressing this letter to you? May be because I don't have anyone else to address to or may be because I am fed up blaming myself and want to put it on someone else. But I am not even sure, if you exist. I am sure of one thing though, you are not dear to me and I was never dear to you either.

You know I have decided to bid adieu to my miserable life. Some lives are such, they are given birth to wander without any purpose or destiny. Then they perish into some unknown darkness without anyone noticing, without leaving a mark behind. My life has been one such story. So, without waiting for the destiny to play any more cruel jokes on me, I have decided to take hold of my destiny and end this painful suffering. I am longing to meet my Uppa and tell him how much I had missed his love and protection.

May be the world will consider me a coward. May be the world will say I should have fought harder. May be the world would tag me as a weak soul. May be this decision will reinstate the common belief of all the prejudiced people around me, that I am a loser. May be… but what do they know of me, and why would I even bother of what 'may be's they have about me.

I found no supporting hand when I fell. The only one alive person for whom I was important was my mother. I had left her long back and now, she has left me forever. I never knew or cared if she loved me. But don't know why, I miss her today; at this very moment, I miss her…

I MISS YOU AMMA.

I am going back to her. I promise, I would be a good son up there. I hope, up there she would be exclusively mine and I would take good care of her.

Ramesh, I tried my best to forget him, not to mention him here, but I realise that I still have not forgiven him and never will. He should not have come into our lives as a 'saviour'; he is the destroyer of my peace.

I never knew what I wanted from life. I had no real ambition; just wanted to be rich in some truthful way. I never had any true friends. I spent most of my life earning small and saving large for no real reason. Now, I realise that I don't have anything of my own. Everything I thought I had were never mine.

Maya! I wish I could forget her and move on with my life. But how could I ? I failed again. I believed she was the angel that you had sent to guide me out of my miseries. I was so wrong just as I was about Gowri. She made me believe there was something more in me than I had ever thought about myself. I had only one reason to be-lieve that it was true; because Maya said so. Now she is nowhere. All of a sudden, she is no one. I have realised that there are no angels. She was never meant to be in my life and has gone forever.

I thought I would write in this letter about how much hate I have towards you, Maya. But I don't want to lie in these last moments of my life. I LOVE YOU MAYA. I hope and pray for you, to be happy wherever you are and succeed in whatever you do. I want you to achieve every dream of yours, reach all the possible heights of success while you chase your passion. Just a request- please don't ever again step on someone's heart to reach the heights, it hurts a lot.

Why does one live? What gives him the strength to continue? What makes him to carry on? HOPE. A hope that good times will come. A hope that one will succeed. A hope that tomorrow will be definitely be better than what today is. A hope that past could be buried somewhere deep and a new present will blossom over it. Isn't that naive? What happens when one loses that hope? You cease to exist. I too have ceased to exist and I am too tired now- to try, to cry, to shout, to fight or to even breath...

I QUIT

Never Yours Ever Neglected,

Kuttan

***

Kuttan folded the letter neatly into four and kept it under the phone. He set an alarm at 11:55 pm. He stared at the door again to make sure no one was watching. He hid himself in the soft furred blanket which she had gifted him. He could not sleep, he lay motionless. He thought of his life until then and wondered if there was something more to his life, beyond what he could see, beyond what he knew.

He had lied about hope. He hoped that the doorbell would ring.

Chapter 33

The Humanoid

'Tring- trong,' rang the doorbell.

It rang again followed by an eternal silence.

Kuttan woke up looking at the roof with reddened eyes. He looked at the clock in the phone, the suicide note was still beneath it, neatly folded. The time was 12:00 am. He had missed the alarm. Did he forget unknowingly or did he forget wilfully?

Twenty nine years back he was born in this world exactly at the same time. He didn't have a say then, this time it was different. He had decided his fate; bloody cheat, she ditched him again! But, this time he didn't complain. He hoped.

With the hope of seeing Maya lighting his way, Kuttan slowly moved towards the front door; step by step, beat by beat and breathe by breathe. He opened the door, no one was there except a bouquet of red roses with a small card. He bent down and opened the card which read;

'For the most precious possession of my life,

Happy Birthday!!!'

Kuttan sensed someone standing behind him, he turned around swiftly.

"Surprise!" said the mesmerising voice he had died to hear,

'almost'. It was followed by a thrust of chocolate cake on to his face.

"Where…?" Kuttan choked due to unexpected exceedingly overt happiness. Kuttan was in tears, thanks to the dark fresh cream cake, which was not evident.

"I know you have many questions for me but first give me a hug, my birthday boy," Maya hugged Kuttan tight. She took a bite of the cake on his face, "You taste so yummy. I feel like eating you, bite after bite."

Kuttan didn't say anything. He just held her tight, tears flowing over the chocolate on his face.

All of a sudden, Kuttan realised that the stupid letter was there in his room. What would Maya think if she read it? He hurried in to the room disregarding her fading voice in the back ground. The note was not there, it had flown out somewhere. Thank God. He would find and tear it down later.

"Where were you? I got so worried? Searched for you everywhere," Kuttan said trying to hide his disappointment beneath slow controlled breathing.

"Everywhere? I don't think so. If you had then you would have found me. You must have stopped the search mid-way somewhere, without trusting," Maya took a sip of wine she had brought, "Ok, no more suspense. I had gone to Paris. I have got the scholarship, they liked my project so much that they are willing to give me fifty percent rebate on fees. Not just that, I can finish the course anytime in next three years. Isn't that wonderful? I can be with you, we can start our company and once you are settled I can go and finish the course," her zeal was evident in her body language.

"Why didn't you tell me?" Kuttan preferred to ignore her excitement.

"I had called you over phone once when you were in Kerala, your step-dad, Ramesh, had attended the call. He told me you were performing the last rites for your mother. So, I told him that I was going to Paris and shall be back in a week. Didn't he tell you?"

"No. I don't remember," Kuttan tried to remember the minimal conversation they had. Actually, Ramesh had approached him a couple of times but Kuttan arrogantly refused to converse with him. The arrogance almost caused him his life. "And why was your phone not reachable? I tried to call you so many times," Kuttan's irritation became evident in his changed voice.

"Hey, take it easy. You were worried for my wellbeing. I got it. I am sorry for not letting you know in person. But, I too got busy because I had to reach there in short period. Moreover, you had a great loss to cope with so I thought the best way was to keep you out of all this and let you have your last few memories with mother. Regarding being not reachable, I lost my phone. I had an accident as I was going from Pune airport to home, on my way back from Paris, to get the papers for the loan. I was in hospital for one week. Did you notice the bandage around my left wrist? No! As I said, you didn't search for me everywhere or else you would have known," Maya stood at her place and explained. She too could have been upset at not having him by his side when she needed him. She didn't com-plain, she understood and expected same from him.

A moment of silence prevailed in the air. Kuttan stood, moved towards her and held her hands, "I am so sorry. I missed you very much, so much so that it almost killed me. I realised that I am nothing without you. I love you so much," he sobbed.

"I love you too. You are so delicate at times and the toughest at other times. You are so full of wonders, you just don't realise your worth," Maya rubbed her hands through his hairs.

Kuttan slowly moved his arms under her t-shirt.

"Hmm...and naughty too," she pushed him back. She expressed her desires with a stare in to his eyes and a wicked smile over her pink lips. The wild desire in his eyes reflected in hers.

She removed her t-shirt. Undressed him.

He slowly moved his hands over the curves of her body and kissed her. He lifted her to the bed in his room. He smelled her as if he had forgot her smell. He kissed her all over, first slowly then with vigour again and again; what if he didn't get another chance? An irrelevant thought passed through his mind for no reason, which he preferred to ignore.

He removed her shorts, slid his fingers underneath the black panty that he had always fantasied to see her in. She moaned, smiled, pinched and pleaded. She held him tight between her thighs, so tight that he could not move. He tried to enter her, again and again, but the resistance was too much from inside while she seemed joyful from outside.

He looked in to her, it was too dark inside. He could not see anything. He jumped into the darkness, which was all, sticky and fluid filled. He tried to swim past the darkness which seemed endless. Finally at the far end he saw a tunnel with bright light blinding him. All of a sudden the fluid level begun to rise, he felt suffocated, he struggled to breathe. He tried to swim out of it but the level kept raising. He swam with all his might, a gigantic hand came through the light. He tried to grasp it but slipped and again plunged in to the dark. He could not breathe, he suffocated and was sure to die.

'Tring…tring…tring…tring…'

Kuttan woke up gasping for air. He was wet all over his body. His breaths were racing with his heart beat to outlast one another. The room was dark; except the moonlight, which filtered through the white curtains filling the room through the glass door of balcony. He turned around he looked at the phone and letter with dismay and disbelief.

He looked towards the balcony. He saw a bright white outline of a humanoid shape. A shape which was too familiar to him but had been forgotten long back. His eyes brightened, the light penetrated through his eyes in to the soul. He felt pleasantly warm inside. His body seemed to disobey him, he felt weak. He could not rise from the bed. With great effort he swallowed his spit, moved lips apart and said,

"Uppa."

Chapter 34

The Shape of Conscience

'Uppa,' the way Muslims, in Malayalam, call their father.

A drop of tear rolled out of Kuttan's left eye over his cheek bone down his earlobe. He had wished for his father to be by his side umpteen number of times before, but he never showed up. Now, when everything was about to end, why had he come? Did he come to take Kuttan along with him, to wherever he was?

"I missed you so much *Uppa*. You are here to take me with you. Aren't you?" Kuttan looked at the shape through the corner of his eyes.

"I am sorry son, I don't have such power. I am just a perception of your inner conscience. I have been summoned by you."

"By me?"

"Yes, you were feeling lonely. You wanted me to be by your side, so that you have strength to do the right thing. You needed someone to guide you."

"I needed that person my whole life. Where were you until now?"

"You didn't need me until now. Deep inside you knew and believed that your mother loved you, and prayed for you. You derived strength from the thought, but now since she is gone you felt lonely...

in real. Isn't it?"

"No, that's not true. Why are you trying to solve the unnecessary puzzles of the past when these things doesn't matter anymore?" Kuttan was getting restless. The voice had touched a note too deep inside him to his discomfort which he didn't wish to admit.

"Again, it's not me. It's you my dear. You feel everything is going to end, so you look back and wonder where did you go wrong? You wonder if there is more to you than you knew, but never admitted."

"I don't believe you. You are lying. You can't be my *Uppa*: he would never lie."

"I can take any shape you wish me to. None would lie. One can lie to the whole world, pretend oblivion, but not to self."

Kuttan stopped being restless. He lay still. His breathes slowed down. After a minute of silence, he began to open up to himself from the deepest of his heart.

"I killed you. You died because of my mistake. I am so sorry Uppa."

"That's so unfair to you. You were a small child, you got scared. I was the grown up, I should had been more careful. And, no one blames you for my death, except you."

"Why do we have to suffer so much *Uppa*? Why my life had been so unfair? It knew that I am a weak soul, but still pushed me towards such a terrible fate?"

"Everyone suffers son. Life is difficult at times but not unfair, it's your attitude towards life that makes life what it is. You are not a weak soul. You are the strongest, I believe. But, what is more important; do you believe? I am so proud of you. All are. But are you proud of yourself? You, despite all the troubles had in childhood never gave up, continued to move forward to realise your dream to be something big, and someone important. To earn the right to love and be loved. And now, when you are so close to realising it, are you going to give up?"

"I wish Amma too had felt so. I wish she had loved me," Kuttan cried like the four year old child, tears poured out of his eyes uncontrollably.

"She did love you, more than anyone else. She wanted you to be strong so, she left you free to take your path but, she had always kept a blessed hand over you. You just never realised it the same way as you didn't realise your own strength and success."

"But, she left me for Ramesh."

"She didn't leave you. You left her. She, just like any other human being, like yourself, had the right to love and be loved. She was so young and beautiful when I died, and you were so small. Whatever she did was to protect you. Ramesh might have been cruel to you at times, but he had protected you even if it was for your mother's sake. He loved her very much. Who do you think had untied you from the tree and helped you escape that night? How come the police never chased you? But, you like all others saw only what you wished to see, believed what was convenient for you. You were a child then but now you are a grown up and know how it feels to be in love. You have to let it go my son. You can't live in denial. You have to accept things as they were, as they are and as they would come in the future. Things that were meant to happen, they happened. You can't change them. Everything happens for a reason; that's life, it's beyond our control. You can't do anything about it. Don't do it to yourself. You don't deserve it, and know that your mother deserved better too."

The silence filled the gap between them for few more minutes.

"Maya! I had loved her so much. She too, like Gowri, betrayed, and left me."

"With Gowri, you had spoilt it yourself; admit it, and be relieved of the burden of false grudge. You can never hate her. And Maya? Do you really believe that she had betrayed you? If what she needed was money, she could have taken the trunk and vanished. Why would she take the pain of getting an account started, loan sanctioned and later not even withdraw full money? Such a miniscule testing time and your relation can't stand it, did you really love her? If yes, you have to trust her and believe she would come back. You are worried that she would go to Paris, realise her dream and never come back. What have you done to support her in pursuit of her passion? You can't cage true love my son. Let it go free and if it's meant for you it will definitely come back to you. Remember son! There is always hope. All you have to do is shun your ego and ignorance to find it, to let it find you. I hope and pray that you will find peace."

"But…" Kuttan had many more doubts in mind but the thoughts seemed jigsawed and blurred.

The bright light faded leaving behind the filtered moonlight. The room seemed warmer. The breeze seemed to have settled down, the curtains flowed rhythmically. Kuttan's heart beats and breathes had found peace in each other's companionship to drive him towards his destiny, his dream and to find true love or survive until it finds him.

'Tring…tring…tring…' snoozed the alarm, time was 12:00 am. The time had come for Kuttan to decide.

Chapter 35

The Decision

Kuttan slowly rose from the bed and moved towards the balcony. The time had already exceeded 'his planned time period', which he had set for his miserable life. However, strangely he didn't seem to be upset with it. He didn't feel offended that his fate had outsmarted him again. His miserable life didn't seem as miserable as it seemed few hours ago. The whole set of events seemed to have happened to someone he thought knew very well, but in real was a stranger.

He reached the railings in the balcony and looked down. A drop of sweat traversed down from his forehead over the dorsum of nose and formed a pearl at the tip of nose. It stood still for a second, reflecting the minimal light and doing its best to shine in the darkness, and then fell down in to the deep void of darkness; still reflecting the light, however little.

A trailing fashion plant that Maya had brought from the estate in Kollur and planted in a mud pot, with a wooden stick for support, seemed to have dried in the pot due to neglect, but not dead. Kuttan used to water it until recently but he had forgot about it for the past three weeks. It still survived. It trailed over the railings and attached itself to the walls where there was water seeping from a pipeline. It sprouted new near the source of water and survived until Kuttan could find it again. It didn't give up, it survived.

Kuttan turned around towards the door. He saw his reflection in the glass of the door. Now, he could look in to 'his' eyes, which was not painful anymore. He saw thousands of lights in the background lighting the whole city. The city which rose every morning without fail. It didn't moan over the past night's failures, it offered only one thing to its residents who survived the darkness of night- HOPE.

A hope that today will bring the happiness that yesterday had failed to deliver. A hope that tomorrow will be better than what today is.

Many voices kept repeating themselves in his mind, all at the same time, overlapping one over another. He could not make out 'who had said what and when', but he could definitely hear them ringing in his ears, occupying his thoughts:

"Remember son! There is always hope. All you have to do is shun your ego and ignorance to find it, to let it find you."

"Then don't try to possess them, just love them."

"Remember son, all the answers to your queries and miseries lie within you, in your past. You just have to look back and think where you went wrong. Don't forget the path that had lead you this far."

"The biggest strength of a man was his belief in the 'self' and biggest weakness was the greed to have more than what he deserved."

"Life is never meant to be easy son. It's your attitude towards the life that makes all the difference."

"You just have to look back and think where you went wrong."

"Never forget the path that had lead you up there to the happiness. That will help you regain it, if lost."

"I hope and pray that you will find peace."

For reason not known to self Kuttan remembered the first day at the college when his professor asked him to introduce himself to the class. He had failed to answer then. He didn't know the right answer. He felt as if the same question the whole world, standing behind, was asking him,

"Who are you?"

Now, he knew the answer, an answer he believed in.

"I am Dileep, my parent's beloved Kuttan. An ordinary man with extraordinary zeal. A fighter who shall not give up. A child who deserves better for himself from the world. A dreamer who has a long struggle ahead to realise his dreams; who shall not rest until he gets there, today or tomorrow," he turned and silently shouted back at the world through his determined eyes. He tore the letter apart and flew it in the air.

Kuttan heard fluttering of wings, something flew into the darkness.

***

Kuttan dialled the phone number.

"Hello! Kuttan?" asked Ramesh. He sounded tired.

Kuttan didn't reply. Ramesh spoke as if he had been waiting for this call, all the past nights.

"I was thinking about your mother. On this day she would go to temple without fail and perform a *pushpanjali*. She would cook *payasam* and distribute among the poor children. Later, in the night she would sob alone. I would let her, I knew no words could console her. She loved you very much Kuttan!" after a brief pause he continued, "Are you there?"

Still Kuttan didn't reply. Ramesh could hear the heaviness of breath trying to penetrate his impermeable egoistic lips, to let out the words that had been trapped within since eternity.

"I am glad that you came; she could finally find peace. Poor creature, she had suffered a lot. I am sorry for your loss but I too have lost someone very precious. I don't know if you would believe or not. I don't even know why I always wanted to tell you this. I loved your mother very much, more than anyone could imagine, maybe more than myself."

The most difficult thing is to realise that you were wrong, even tougher is to admit it, only strong people could do it.

"I am sorry... Ramesh...*mama*. Thank you for loving my mother so much, thank you for taking good care of her," with lots of effort

Kuttan laid rest to the demons within and relieved his soul from an invisible load that he didn't know existed, an obstacle to his spirited flight.

"One more thing I need to tell you. I don't know if it is important but felt that you should know. I should have told earlier but, you didn't wish to hear my voice," Ramesh sighed, "That day, when you were performing the funeral rites for your mother, a girl had called. I attended the call. I tried to tell you but you arrogantly refused to talk and moved away. I was so upset with you later that I didn't try to speak again, I too had a great loss to cope with. She told me that she was going to Paris, it was very urgent, and would return soon."

"I know. It's not your mistake, you need not be sorry. Everything happens for a reason. Everything around us is just the reflection of our life: the *Samsara*..." Kuttan smiled and disconnected the phone. A smile of a man content with himself, who was sure of his destiny.

'Tring-trong', rang the doorbell.

***

Epilogue

One year later.

Kuttan stood in a wet towel at the *Papanasam* beach (the destroyer of sins) in Varkala, Kerala. Bright morning sun shined, adding to the bluish hue of the horizon. The waves were calm washing off the offerings of the *balikarma* from the shore; the waves along with them washed off the sufferings and sins of the departed souls enabling them eternal relief- *Moksha*.

In front of Kuttan lay the banana leaf with rice ball and sesames seeds offering. Ramesh stood beside him in silence.

"I think we should move away, let *her* have the offering in peace," Kuttan suggested to Ramesh, who sighed and moved back with an affirmative head movement.

Kuttan looked at the crow sitting at a distance which watched Kuttan throughout the *balikarma*. He felt it had compassion in its eyes. He looked at the crow for one last time, turned back and walked over the white sand leaving his trail only to be washed away by some unknown tide sooner or later. A few distance away he turned back; the crow ate the offering, it didn't look at him. She need not. Her son had found peace and contentment; he didn't need her protection anymore.

"She would surely be at peace and very proud of you. Wherever she might be, she would always be watching," said Maya holding Kuttan's hand tight.

"Not just she, my *Uppa* too, like he had always been. They

would watch us together," said Kuttan.

Kuttan smiled looking at the bright blue sky, like a four year old child, tracing cloud patterns. There he saw a beautiful boat, which held and showered blessings of his *Uppa* and Amma.

Acknowledgement

Thank You. I am thankful to you for reading my book. This story transformed from a vague idea, generated over a casual conversation, into the book you just finished. But, this book came into existence because of help and support of many people, and without mentioning them, my story would not be complete.

Thank you Bindiya and Pankaj for your unconditional support for my writing.

Thank you Jayalakshmi for correcting so many obvious mistakes which I didn't notice. Your untiring corrections made the book what it is now.

Thank you Mini Raj and Deepthi Ajit for reading the first draft, and telling me honestly that it was not up to the mark.

Thank you my family and son, Ayan for your love and smile, they are my stress busters.

Thank you Shabu Prasad for the timely suggestions and guidance regarding submissions and publishing.

Thank you Manik Jaiswal for your opinions and inputs about publishing.

I am thankful to the whole team of Saikatham Books for believing in my writing, and giving me the opportunity to work with you. Thank you for all the efforts you have put in to make this dream a reality.

And, as said earlier, I am thankful to the unknown Universal

Power which energises us to continue the journey in pursuit of our dreams.